JIM STEEL: GOLD TRAIN

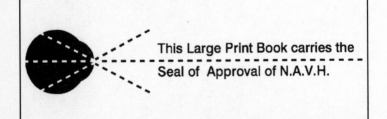

This Large Print Book carries the
Seal of Approval of N.A.V.H.

JIM STEEL: GOLD TRAIN

CHET CUNNINGHAM

WHEELER PUBLISHING
A part of Gale, Cengage Learning

Detroit • New York • San Francisco • New Haven, Conn • Waterville, Maine • London

GALE
CENGAGE Learning™

Copyright © 1981 by Chet Cunningham.
Wheeler Publishing, a part of Gale, Cengage Learning.

LIBRARY OF CONGRESS CATALOGING-IN-PUBLICATION DATA

Cunningham, Chet.
    Jim Steel : gold train / by Chet Cunningham.
      p. cm. — (Wheeler Publishing large print western)
    ISBN-13: 978-1-4104-3184-4 (softcover)
    ISBN-10: 1-4104-3184-3 (softcover)
    1. Gold theft—Fiction. 2. Large type books. I. Title. II. Title:
Gold train.
PS3553.U468J57 2010
813'.54—dc22   2010030436

Published in 2010 by arrangement with Chet Cunningham.

Printed in the United States of America
1 2 3 4 5 6 7 14 13 12 11 10

JIM STEEL: GOLD TRAIN

PROLOGUE

Ask almost anyone in the western half of the United States in the year of 1869 and the name of Jim Steel would be known. Most people could tell you he was known as the Gold Man. He never tried for the title, but more and more those who lived beyond the Missouri heard about his exploits and every one of his adventures had at its center . . . GOLD!

In that year of 1869 there was little else to catch the imagination of a surging and growing nation. On March 4, 1869 General Ulysses S. Grant was sworn in as the eighteenth President. Much more important to those beyond the Colorado line was the pounding of the final spike in the transcontinental railroad on May 10 at Promontory Point, Utah, when the Union Pacific and the Central Pacific tracks met and bound the nation together with steel rails.

Women rejoiced when they won the right

to vote in the Territory of Wyoming that year. Then on September 13, 1869 Jay Gould and James Fisk tried to get into Jim Steel's act by cornering the gold market. The government dumped gold on the market to stabilize the price. Jim Steel hardly noticed the gold problems or Black Friday. He wasn't a politician although he did serve as an elected sheriff for a time in Kansas and one time in Arizona. But he wasn't happy as a lawman, especially after he was tried for murder while he was still wearing a badge. He beat the charge, but never pinned on a star again.

Instead he turned to mining, putting in a year in a hard rock gold quartz hole, then moved on to the silver mines. At last he realized that he didn't have to dig gold out of a mountain. Others could dig it, the important thing was who owned it.

At one time Mid-Pacific Railroad wanted to talk to Jim about a lost gold shipment from a sealed baggage car. Jim was on board the train when the gold turned up missing, and Jim was accused, but charges were never brought and nothing was proved. There was never a wanted poster on Jim Steel.

Some told the story about Jim being in Texas when a bandit cleaned $12,000 in gold from a bank, stopped to kiss two pretty women customers on his way out, and even tipped his hat. Jim was in the same town, but no one could prove he had anything to do with the robbery.

Jim didn't mind the stories. He let them build and grow, and told everyone his conscience was clear. He'd paid his dues in the game, and now he was ready to cash in on the gold business anyway he could — legally. He had no stomach for the Yuma Territorial Prison, or any similar institution.

A few years back Jim had considered hijacking a *GOLD WAGON* that Uncle Sam was sending from California to Washington, D.C. By the time he found the ton of gold on the wagon, he wound up protecting instead of stealing it. In the end he came up with a river of gold dust that nobody would ever recover, but wound up with a few small gold bars for his trouble.

He was tricked into working on the *DIE OF GOLD* adventure. Someone hired him to protect a five-man army patrol moving into the High Sierras with new dies for the gold double eagle coins. But it turned out to be a doublecross and frameup that took on a personal side as hot lead flew by Jim's head.

Everyone in the West knew about gold in Arizona. That meant the fantastic, and most

9

thought fictional, story of the Apache wall of gold. But despite a pair of Eastern dudes and rampaging Chiricahus Apaches, Jim Steel did find the Apache wall of gold and took a few samples out with him and even saved a white girl. But *BLOODY GOLD* was not Jim's most dangerous adventure.

DEVIL'S GOLD found Jim Steel high in the Colorado Rockies trying to discover who had killed a hard rock mine buddy of his at a placer mining show called Devil's Gulch. Before he was done *DEVIL'S GOLD* produced a fine panning operation and soon he found a mother lode which he shared with the widow of his friend when she suddenly turned up in the woman-starved mining camp.

Jim Steel never hunted trouble, but somehow it always found him. The most innocent trip might turn into a hellish ride for his life, and a simple job like shepherding a packet of valuable papers across the country from Denver through the new rail lines to Sacramento should have been a simple and tame affair. Actually it was, but that was only window dressing for the *GOLD TRAIN.*

CHAPTER 1

Jim Steel sat on the cushioned seat of the railroad coach as it lurched and swayed across the still settling bed of the Central Pacific Railroad two days out of Denver. His clear blue eyes were alert, taking in everything around him as if he were still a lead scout on an army patrol. Now his low-crowned gray hat shaded his eyes as he looked down the aisle at the end of the car. Thick black hair crowded out from under the felt, and partially hid both ears, giving him a slightly Indian look. A heavy black mustache and long sideburns accented the leanness of his handsome face. The whiskers helped to protect his skin from the wind and weather at the trail whether it was the desert heat of New Mexico or the icy blasts of a Colorado winter.

He had the look of a man slightly uncomfortable indoors, and the easy way he moved his lean, hard body gave others the idea that he was a wildcat about to pounce. Jim sighed and folded his hands over the leather vest and wondered if he should take a short snooze or go check the baggage car again.

After all, that was what he was getting paid for, to nursemaid a packet of documents across the west to Sacramento and into the hands of a banker there. Not much of a mission and he was sure the whole thing was a waste of time and money, but he had spent all the time he wanted to in Denver anyway, this trip. He'd gone to the opera, and a musical, played poker until he was bored, read a newspaper every day and had bathed daily for almost a week. Now it was time for some movement, some action. He had planned to go out to the silver country in Nevada anyway, and this was on the way, just a hop and a skip over the hill from Sacramento on the train.

From long habit Jim checked the passengers again. In front of him sat a couple from Missouri if he judged the accent right. Then there was a man going to San Francisco to begin a doctor's practice. To the other side sat a pair of newlyweds traveling to San Francisco for their honeymoon. Their desire was to see an ocean.

Behind him was a tall, lean priest, with a turned around white collar and a Bible that was always open, though the priest did not often look at it. The churchman had been a late arrival to the train and Jim got the impression they held up the departure until the holy man arrived. Maybe he had to bless the train on the way in.

Two seats ahead of him was a young girl, with a dress just a bit too fancy for traveling, but she was young, probably not yet twenty-one. She had long brown hair, a round smiling face and a book that she didn't seem to be reading as much as she wanted people to believe. For a moment she turned and stared at Jim, then she looked away. He watched her for a few minutes and saw that she made a habit of looking at each of the passengers, studying them, perhaps.

Jim Steel shrugged, left his seat and walked through the coach to the baggage car immediately behind. He rapped on the window of the baggage car. A moment later the postal clerk and guard unlocked the door and let him in. The safe was in the baggage and mail car. The combination mail clerk, baggage man, and guard had to protect everything. He wore a .44 caliber Centennial Army revolver on his leg tied down low and out of the way.

"Howdy, Pete. Any action?"

"Quiet as a tomb, Mr. Steel. Just the way I like it. I can get my sorting done. I don't allow any other visitors in here but you, orders from the road." He dropped a package of letters wrapped with string, cut the string and began throwing letters into various sacks gaping open on steel holders.

"This job is tough enough without some valuables in the safe. One day we had a gold shipment in there, and I about went to the crazy house."

"No gold this time," Jim assured him. "Just some papers. Looks like they should have put a couple of stamps on the envelope and mailed it. But you know how some of these big companies are."

"Yeah, true, just like the railroad."

Jim turned for the door. "You take care of my baby, Pete."

"Intend to, Mr. Steel."

Jim watched him sort the envelopes and postal cards for a moment, then went back to the section between the cars and watched the country spinning by. He'd ridden over this area more than once on a horse, and averaged about four miles an hour. Now the train was rolling along at more than 30 he was sure, maybe even 35 or 40 miles in one hour. Amazing. And it never had to stop for breath or oats or hay. But it did stop for

14

water and more wood to stoke the boiler's firebox.

Jim could ride 40 miles a day on a horse for a week and feel little pain. This Iron Horse could do 350 to 450 miles in one 24 hour day! The world was simply starting to move too fast. This was no way to enjoy the country, everything flashing past a dirty window. And think of the smoke, soot and ashes that blew right inside the car sometimes.

Jim shrugged and turned to the door with the window in it that led him from the little platform between the cars and then into the passenger coach. Two men inside had guns out and were robbing the passengers. Jim pulled his new weapon from his holster. It was a Ruger Old Army revolver, with a .44 slug and a 7 1/2 inch barrel, with walnut grips, brass backstrap and trigger guard. It weighed almost three pounds and was the most accurate six-gun he had ever fired.

Jim dropped to one knee and slid the door open silently, but the clicky-clack of the steel wheels on the track joints caused the first gunman to look up and swing his gun around.

Jim's first shot up the clear aisle took the robber high in the chest and slapped him backwards, his weapon falling away as the man screamed and hit the floor. The roar of Jim's .44 brought a scream from a woman nearby and a second one fainted. The robber at the other end of the car dove between seats and out of Jim's sight line.

Jim ran into the car and slid behind the first seat. He wondered if the seat cushion would stop a .44 from close range, and doubted it. Nobody moved in the car. There were about twenty passengers spread around. Jim lifted his head to look over the seats and saw that everyone had dropped down to the seats or the floor for safety. Jim saw only the top of a black Stetson near the next to last seat as it vanished.

Nobody said a word.

"It's just you and me, pardner," Jim called loudly. "Throw out your gun and I promise not to ventilate your chest like I did your ex-buddy back here. Toss it out, now!"

The voice from down the car didn't seem impressed.

"Not so, stranger. I've got a trump ace in the hole you don't know about."

With that the man stood and Jim's gun came up but stopped when he saw the girl that the robber pulled up to cover himself. It was the pretty girl with the book she wasn't reading.

"Now, smartass, you just drop your hogleg in the aisle and I won't put a chunk of hot lead through this little girl's pretty face. You hear me, stranger?"

Jim laughed. "Hell, I don't know her from Jane Doe or Martha Washington. That's a bluff that won't work. You gun her down and you're wide open and I got no excuse for missing you with six slugs right in your gut. Now, take your choice. I got all the way to the next stop at Roundtop for water, before I make my move."

The man wavered and Jim saw it. Most outlaws even in desperate situations would not harm a woman. There were too few women in the West and pretty ones were a premium. The gunman backed slowly toward the door, taking the girl with him.

"You stay put, stranger," the robber called. At the door he slid out and pushed the girl back into the car he had just left.

As soon as the girl was free, Jim was up and running down the aisle, stepping over the dead man on the floor. As he neared the door the glass window in it shattered and Jim had time only to lunge to one side to escape the hot lead and flying glass.

The gunman had continued into the next passenger car, the last one. Jim raced after him, then looked into the car, but could not see the man through the glass door.

He opened the door, bent over low and rushed into the car to the first seat. A man of about fifty with eyes that sparkled with excitement sat near the window in the seat. He bent his head below the seat back.

"The Jasper you're hunting is almost at the far end. Ran in here with a gun just after that shot. He don't know it but he can't get out the other door. It's locked cause it backs up to the engine and the coal car."

"Thanks." Jim checked to see that the other passengers had their heads down. "All right, you with the gun," Jim called. "You're trapped. That door is locked behind you and there's no way out except through me. You ready to talk?"

"Is Logan dead?" a voice asked.

"If Logan is the jayhawker who was robbing those folks in the other car, he ain't feeling none too chipper. Dead I don't know about."

"I could shoot down half a dozen people in here before you took me out," the robber said. "I could make you pay for what it cost me."

"True, you could do that, and you could die yourself when your ammo ran out. Think about it. If you get yourself killed, you're going to be dead for one hell of a long time."

"What you offering?"

"You didn't hurt anybody, far as I can tell. Reckon I'd go along with putting you and your friend off at the next stop. But that's up to the conductor. He's the boss on this contraption, at least for the passengers."

"You go get him, he's in the other car, so scared he can't stand up. You go get that spitless wonder."

"Lift that iron of yours straight up and point it at the roof while I leave," Jim said. He saw the weapon rise from behind a seat and aim for the top of the coach. Only then did Jim back carefully through the door and into the next car.

A minute later Jim had the conductor up to the first coach. He argued with Jim about the situation.

"I'm bound by company regulations to hold any perpetrators of serious crimes for the police in the next jurisdiction," the conductor said.

Jim smiled. "Then the passengers will have to testify and talk to the sheriff and a report will go back to Central Pacific, and it will look pretty bad, won't it? It will have to read something like this: 'The conductor did nothing to prevent the robbery of passengers. The conductor cowered in a seat unable to stand and did not pull the emergency cord to stop the train, did not offer resistance to the robbers in any respect.' Now, that's not going to look good on your employment record, is it?"

The conductor took off his stiff billed, black cap and wiped sweat off his forehead. His eyes came up, pleading.

"So what else can I do?"

"It isn't your fault if a robber attacks the train. One gets killed in the melée and then the desperados escape. I'd say we should pitch them both off the train at the first upgrade."

The conductor, a fat man in his late forties, smiled weakly and nodded. "Yes, that's it. And I don't thank many of the people lost things. I mean maybe we can get back the cash and jewelry."

From the other end of the car the robber spoke.

"Well, what the hell you two decide? Do we shoot it out, or what?"

Jim motioned for the conductor to talk. They both crouched behind a seat. The other man could not be seen.

"It seems we have a standoff here. The railroad will allow you and your friend to depart the train at the next upgrade. We'll help your friend detrain. All we ask is that you return the money and valuables you took so far."

"Not on your life! This has been a waste of time anyway."

They all felt the train slow as it came to a rise.

"You can do anything you want to with Chuck. I'm getting off right here." He backed to the door, remembered that it was locked, then came toward the other two, his gun still out.

Jim had his weapon ready, held loosely.

"I'd suggest, pardner, that you lower the muzzle of that hogsleg or I'm going to lift mine."

The robber, a man of about thirty, with a full beard, nodded. He pulled his hat lower on his head, kept his face turned as he passed the two, then spun around and backed out the door. They could see him between the cars for a moment, then he looked back, waved, and leaped between the cars and off the train.

Jim went back to the first coach and checked the man he'd shot. He was dead. Jim and the conductor carried the body to the nearest door and between the cars, then Jim threw the body down the side of the right of way.

"I really don't like doing this," the conductor said, wiping more sweat off his forehead.

"Yeah, life is tough. But just remember, he wouldn't have minded tossing your lifeless body off here. With just a little bad luck that could be you laying out there in the weeds and rocks with a bullet in your forehead."

The conductor sucked in a quick breath, wiped some sweat from his black billed cap, and put it on. He cleared his throat, then shook his head.

"Well, yes. Now, I guess I better find out how much money and valuables were stolen. I'm in for a stack of paper work that I really don't like."

Jim laughed. "You're alive, man. Be glad you can still make your pencil work."

Back in the coach, Jim settled down in the seat by the window he had used before. He had just slid his low-crowned gray hat down over his eyes when he saw a floor-length skirt and then a young lady sit in the seat beside him.

"Sir?"

He wondered if he should pretend to be sleeping. The voice was young and he recognized the skirt as the one worn by the pretty young girl who had been the gunman's short-time captive and shield.

Slowly he pushed back his hat and sat up straighter as he turned to look at her. She was prettier than he had thought, with soft creamy skin, darting brown eyes, long brown hair that sparkled in the light. There was a touch of fragrance about her that he couldn't pin down. Her nose was short and slightly tipped upward over pink lips that parted to show shining white teeth. Her dress covered her up to her chin and a series of small buttons marched down the front over firm young breasts to a tiny waist.

She had been looking him over as he had inventoried her and they both smiled. Dimples cut into her soft cheeks.

"I'm sorry, Miss. I didn't mean to stare, but I always end up staring at the prettiest girl in the room, or on the train."

No blush touched her throat, instead she smiled as if it were what she expected to hear.

"I just wanted to thank you for saving my life. You were there and made him let me go, and he didn't shoot me or anything. I didn't even have a chance to get my derringer out of my reticule. Daddy says I shouldn't carry the gun, but I'm certainly glad I did. For a minute there I thought I should take it out and shoot him before he grabbed me, but then it was too late. And I know I'm talking too much and we haven't even been introduced, but you just saved my life and I figure that it's all right if we talk."

She took a deep breath and he laughed softly. She was so lovely he couldn't believe it. A combination of high cheek bones, soft skin and piercing eyes that caught him off guard.

He tipped his hat. "Thank you, Miss. My name is Steel, Jim Steel, and it was an honor to help out any way I could, especially to rescue such a beautiful lady."

She grinned, a little girl's grin, and then giggled. "I'm Mandy Martin. How do you do?" She smiled up at him. "My goodness, you're so full of sweet talk a person would think you were coming courting or something."

"Well now, Miss. That wouldn't quite be proper, would it?"

"I'm not at all worried about being proper, Mr. Steel. But I do thank you for not shooting me, or letting that robber shoot me. And I think it was very gallant the way you acted and I want you to understand that."

"Yes, Miss. I do, and I thank you."

"So, just like that? That's all there is to it?" She frowned. "You kill a man saving me and then . . ."

"Miss, I shot the man before you were in

any danger. Don't make it quite so dramatic."

She scowled. He much preferred her smile.

"May I sit here for the rest of the trip?"

"Seat's open, and I'm sure you have a ticket. If you'll pardon me, I have to go check on something."

"Where are you going?"

"Baggage car."

"Why? What's in there? I've seen you go back there half a dozen times in the past two days."

"Nothing for you to worry about." Before he left he pushed the spent cartridge from his sixgun and put in the replacement, making sure the hammer was resting on the empty chamber.

"You really do use those. I thought the rounds in your belt might just be for decoration."

"Yes, Miss, I really use them. Now excuse me." He slid past her and felt her knees push out to brush against his legs as he left. When he looked back she was still smiling at him. Jim walked to the baggage car and knocked on the door. The clerk opened it.

"Hear you had some excitement up there."

"Some, Pete."

"None back here. Think I might leave the

postal service and become a railroad detective. You guys have all the fun."

"And we get shot at. I'm not a railroad man. I'm private. Just checking this envelope through for a friend. For my banker, matter of fact. He told me he might not give me any more credit if I didn't."

"So you get squeezed into a job you really didn't want. Know how you feel. I wanted to be a doctor. So here I am trying to read the crazy handwriting people have. You ever tried to tell a 'C' from a 'G' on a letter?"

"Afraid not, Pete. The safe, has it been opened?"

"Not since we left Denver, Mr. Steel."

"Good."

Jim turned and headed back to his seat. He couldn't see what was so confounded important about a few sheets of paper. Even if they were stocks or bonds of some kind. He decided not to worry about it, and at the same time he hoped the girl was gone when he got back. She was young, too young, and he didn't want to get involved with a girl like her. While he was on the job he couldn't afford to have any distractions, no matter how pretty she was.

On the way back to his seat, Jim bumped into the priest who was just getting up. The Bible went one way, hornrimmed eyeglasses the other way and the priest dropped back on the seat.

The lean, tall priest scowled for a moment, then a smile covered his face and he stood.

"Sorry, I bumped into you, young man. I should have looked before I moved."

"No, Father. It was my fault. Please, you go ahead." As the priest left the seat Jim had a good look at him. To his surprise the man wore a slight fragrance, shaving lotion probably, and his fingernails had been manicured recently. The man's face was thin, almost gaunt and his eyes were a soft green with flecks of gray. Then he was gone up the aisle and Jim continued to his seat.

The girl, Mandy, still sat where he had left her.

"The conductor says we'll be in Sacramento in five more hours," Mandy said, smiling.

He pushed past her and settled into the seat, then looked at her.

"Good," he said in response, then leaned back, pulled the hat over his eyes and folded his arms on his chest.

"Hey, aren't you even going to talk to me?" Mandy asked in a low voice.

"Nope,"

"You're infuriating, you know that! You

save my life and then you won't even talk with me. Can't you tell I'm frightened?"

"You were about as frightened as a Pony Soldier on parade just before a week-end leave."

"At least you could be polite and talk."

"Yes, Miss."

"So talk."

"I thought we were talking."

"No, you're grumping and trying to be sullen. I could tickle you, that would liven you up."

He pushed the hat up, his eyes locking with hers, but she didn't look away or back down.

Jim laughed softly. "I think you really would. And that's going to get you in trouble someday. But it won't be by me. I probably won't see you again after we get to Sacramento."

"Hey, want a sandwich? I bought some at that last stop. They look like ham and cheese, and I've got two apples. Want to have a picnic?"

Jim laughed. "Why the hell not?"

She giggled and the dimples came back. "Why the hell not? Now that's the way I like to hear you talk. I'll be right back." She jumped from the seat and ran forward and in a few moments she was back with a small picnic basket. She put it between them, opened it and pointed.

"Oh, I forgot. I've got two bottles of beer too. But then I don't suppose you drink beer."

"Only when I'm alone or with somebody."

She laughed and he liked the sound.

"Are you married?"

It always came. This time he nodded. "Yep, and we've got ten kids."

She frowned. "You aren't that old."

"Sure I am. And I have three more kids on the way. Three wives, all pregnant. Like to keep them that way. We're Mormons out of Salt Lake."

She stared at him for a moment, serious, then she grinned, the dimples came and she giggled.

"You are spoofing me, Mr. Steel, I can tell now. And you don't even wear a wedding band."

"Rings? We wear rings. One in each ear and a third in our noses. Don't you see them?"

They both laughed and she gave him a sandwich as he opened a bottle of beer.

"That's naughty making fun of another man's religion."

"True, but it seemed like a good idea at the time," he said.

He ate the sandwich, then pushed forward. "I've got to go play mother hen for a minute."

"What?"

"Be right back."

Jim checked the baggage car again, talked to Pete and went back to the seat beside Mandy. She had moved to the window.

"Make it easier for you to get in and out," she said and handed him the rest of his bottle of beer.

Jim took a pull on the beer and felt like he was loafing on the job. He was getting paid $200 for shepherding this package, and it felt like a fool's errand. It was too simple. When was the train going to explode, or derail? But somehow he knew that nothing would happen. The whole thing had the feeling of a practice run, and he couldn't shake the idea. Then he looked back at the pretty girl beside him chattering away. He figured that the trip would soon be over, then he could head back to Virginia City and that silver mine he wanted to look at.

"Now I think you're going to like Sacramento, Jim. It's not as big as Denver, not as sophisticated and all that, but we have a newspaper, and a couple of good mines, and lots of stores."

Jim took the next sandwich she handed

him and concentrated on enjoying the scenery of the High Sierras as the train began to climb in earnest again. He would watch this pretty young girl and talk and laugh with her all the way to Sacramento. Then this job would be over and he could get on with his own life.

CHAPTER 2

When a train pulled in at the Sacramento Union Pacific Railroad station it was still an event. A hundred persons crowded the platform, looking at the giant steam engine, marveling at the cars rolling so quietly along the steel rails. The conductor put down a step and the passengers filed off.

Sacramento hadn't changed much in the two years since Jim had been there last. A stark, rough, exuberant frontier town with serious growing pains. There were close to 15,000 people living there now Jim had heard, and everything had exploded in a surge of enthusiasm, money, and dreams.

No one met Jim and he didn't expect anyone. He had visited the baggage car an hour before, taken the papers from the safe and had the clerk tape the envelope to his back under his shirt. He pushed the cotton shirt back in place, put on his vest and his lightweight jacket, then went back to the coach. He saw nothing suspicious as the train rolled into town, or at the station. Jim looked around a moment at the people on the platform made of rough-sawed two-by-twelve planks, then walked quickly toward the bank. It was just after two o'clock, the bank would be open.

"SACRAMENTO FIRST STATE BANK" boasted the sign over the door. Jim pushed the panel open and stepped inside. He could never get used to the smell in a bank. They all shared a distinctive odor that he could never identify. It couldn't be anything to do with the coinage, perhaps it was only the musty one hundred dollar bills that smelled.

There were three metal teller's cages with worried looking young men in dark suits behind them. To the left were offices and in front of them stood a desk where a mannish-looking woman sat staring at him. He approached her.

"I'd like to see Mr. Ambrose Smith."

She half smiled but it wasn't really a smile, more of a smirk.

"Mr. Smith is president of this bank and he's a very busy man. Perhaps you could come back tomorrow?"

"No, ma'am, I don't reckon I could. That seems to be his door right there."

Jim took three long strides and he was at the fancy oak door marked with Smith's name, and turned the ornate knob.

"You can't simply barge in there!" the woman protested from the safety of her desk.

"Miss, you just watch me," Jim said and walked into the office.

A man sat behind a polished oak desk smoking a cigar and talking with a poorly dressed man with fringes of hair around a bald plate. The man looked up quickly, then glanced away from the newcomer as the banker stood.

"Ah, yes. You must be Jim Steel. Heard you arrived and were coming to see me. Glad to meet you." He waved the other man out a side door and came around the desk, his hand out to Jim.

"I see you made the trip just fine, Steel. You have the goods?"

"Yes, Mr. Smith, and I'd like to dump them and get on with my own business. You have a paper I'm supposed to sign and mail back, a receipt."

"Oh, I'm afraid I'm not the one who can sign. No, those papers must be hand delivered in person by you directly to Harvey C. Martindale at the Lucky Seven mine. He's the owner. The papers are his. This was just a way point on your trip. I've got a rig ready, or if you prefer a good horse, I've got a pair standing by."

Jim pursed his lips and snorted. "I understood I was to deliver the papers here. Those were my instructions. That sounds good enough for me. If you want them out at some mine, it's your job to take them there."

Smith chuckled. "They told me you could be a hardcase. Matter of fact, your pay envelope is out at the Lucky Seven. It's the only way you get paid for your trouble, so why don't we just relax, have a smoke and then ride out there?" He offered Jim a long brown cigar. Jim had taken to using an occasional cheroot again. He couldn't resist. Another few hours. He shrugged.

Two more men rode with them on horseback. When he found out the mine was seven miles out of town he snorted again. He had been sitting on a bench too long, so chose one of the saddled horses. His was a white stallion with a small black star between his eyes. He was a strong animal, and Jim figured he could outrun anything he'd seen lately.

They angled through some flatlands, over two small streams, then up a valley that eventually led to another smaller valley, and at last upward into a canyon where Jim saw a hard rock mine layout. From what he could see it was a normal working gold mine: holes, tailings, a stamping plant and the rest of the operation that turned raw ore into gold bars.

It was nearly five in the afternoon when they arrived. They had talked little. Jim either rode ahead or behind the buggy which Smith drove. He wanted to be alone for a little bit. He had felt trapped and cramped on the train.

They stopped at a large log cabin, which he found out was more than a simple cabin. Inside it was the mine office and also living quarters for the owner. It was a big place, the front two stories high and with offices and rooms at the back. They were met on the wide porch by Martindale. He was a small man, about five feet four, with pure white hair, clean shaven except for mutton-chop sideburns. Jim put his age at about forty-five. He wore spectacles and a suit and vest with shiny patent leather shoes that he must have had polished every morning. A gold chain linked his vest pockets and in the middle hung a gold nugget the size of a robin's egg.

"And you must be Jim Steel," Martindale said as Jim got down from his horse. He held out his hand to Jim and the grip was surprisingly strong. "Glad to meet you, very glad to meet you. Come in and we'll all have a drink and toast you for your safe trip."

"Well thank you, Mr. Martindale. I'd just like to give you the papers, get the receipt and be on my way."

"I understand. Busy men can't be lolly-gagging around. Know just what you mean. Smith, let's get this thing moving."

They went inside and to a corner where a huge fireplace dominated the room, and where sat a desk with a broken leg that had been put back on with a nailed splint. The top was cigarette-scarred and had a knife or axe wound in it that would never heal. Martindale sat on the front edge of the desk.

"Oh, this is my long-time partner, my very first desk. Been with me for some thirty years now, and never once has let me down. Now, the papers?"

Jim pulled his shirt from his pants and took it off showing the papers taped to his back. Martindale laughed as he pulled the packet loose, unsealed it and studied the material inside for a moment. "Yes, everything is here." He pushed a stack of fifteen freshly minted twenty-dollar gold pieces at Jim, who took ten, and dropped them in his pocket, ignoring the rest.

"Thank you, Mr. Martindale, it's been a

pleasure. I never did quite understand this little trip. But my banker in Denver said it was important. I hope it was worth the cost. Now, if you'll excuse me, I have some other fish to fry."

"You're more than welcome to stay for supper and bunk down here for the night, Jim," Martindale said. "It's a long ride back to town. Why don't you stay, and in the morning I can give you a guided tour of the mine? I understand you've spent some time underground yourself and in the management end of mining."

"My banker has a big mouth," Jim said smiling. "No, I think I better be moving on."

They walked toward the door.

A girl came from the other side of the wide front room. She had brown hair piled on top of her head in some Paris fashion, and wore a long Chinese dress. She stared at the men through large, dark colored glasses. Then she screamed and ran toward them.

"How dare you come here! You brute! You monster! How could you show up here after what you did!" She charged Jim and began beating at him with small, ineffective fists. Jim caught one hand, then the other. She kept yelling at him as he tried to calm the girl. He thought something about her was familiar, but he couldn't quite tie it down.

"Daddy, you remember my telling you about my terrible train ride. How this man got familiar with me and then at night tried to pull my clothes off and rape me? This is the man on the train who did it! He tried to rape me! I'll never forget his face. I want you and these men to hang him right this instant!"

CHAPTER 3

Jim felt a wave of anger, but stifled it before it could show on the surface. Why was she doing this? There had to be some reason for a stranger to come up to him and explode. With the large dark glasses he could see little of her face, and her hair piled up that way. . . .

Harvey C. Martindale's face clouded and he caught the girl's arm and pulled her away from Jim, quieting her. He stood between the girl and Jim.

"Sir, I think you and I better have a long talk. This is a serious charge." He looked at the others. "No need for you gentlemen to stay. This looks to be a matter of — what should we say — a family affair. You can go on your way assured that I will handle the situation. If I don't get the right answers, Mr. Steel here will be either married or hanged come morning. Thanks for coming out, Ambrose, I'll be in touch."

Jim took a step toward Martindale.

"Now wait a minute, you have no cause —"

Martindale pointed a derringer at Jim, the small ugly twin .45 caliber barrels unwavering. He looked at Jim with a scowl of anger. The girl moved back another step, and stared at her father with delight.

The bankers walked toward the front door. Jim looked down at the derringer and knew it would be foolish to try to make any kind of a move now.

"I suggest we go over by the fireplace and have our talk," Martindale said as the banker went out the door. The man looked back, shook his head, and kept going.

Jim and Martindale walked toward the fireplace and the older man pointed to a chair and told Jim to sit down. He took an upholstered chair and the girl sat on the arm. She seemed to be smiling now. He wished she would take off the glasses so he could get a good look at her.

They heard the horses leave outside and Harvey C. Martindale grinned and then chuckled. He tossed the derringer to Jim.

"It's not loaded," he said. "I had to make it look good but I didn't want to risk shooting you."

"Make it look good?" Jim parroted.

The girl unpinned her hair and let the long brown flow spread out over her shoulders, then she took off her dark glasses and smiled. Twin dimples punctured soft cheeks.

"Mandy Martin, the girl on the train," Jim said and scowled. "Would Martin be short for Martindale by any chance?"

"Yep," Mandy said.

"And you were on the train to spy on me."

"Not exactly spying, evaluating would be a better word. We did want to see how you handled yourself on the mission and see what you did if anything untoward took place."

"You set up the train robbery?"

"Oh, goodness, no. That was serendipity. We'd never risk lives with anything like that. It did work out rather well though when I saw how you clobbered those two robbers. And I might add that Daddy and I think you passed your test with an outstanding score. Congratulations."

Jim tossed the derringer back to Martindale. "A test? The whole thing was a phony trip just so you could test me? I had enough of those dry run practices in the army to last a lifetime." He took out the ten double eagles and tossed them to Martindale who caught all but two. He left the others lying where they fell.

"Here's your money back. I didn't do anything to earn it. And like I said before, I've got other fish to fry."

"Hold on, Steel. You keep the money. You did the job you were hired for. Those documents you brought were valuable and I needed them in a rush. It also proved to me you can take on the next job that I want to offer you."

"You don't hear very well, Martindale. There's a silver mine over to Silver City that's up for sale and I just might be able to buy it. I'm leaving."

"No, Mr. Steel, I don't think so. Everyone knows Mandy went to Denver and that she came back on the same train you did. And I've got three upstanding citizens as witnesses who heard Mandy accuse you of attempted rape. You try to ride away from here and I'll bring in six guards with guns, and put you under citizen's arrest. This is my town, Steel. I can see that you get twenty years in prison."

"With a trial or just on your say?"

"Mr. Steel, fair and square, a trial and judge and everything. I'll also furnish the testimony, the witnesses and the jury. It's my town, son, no way you can fight that."

Jim sat down. "If it means that kind of trouble up front, I can at least listen to your proposition."

"Good. I thought I had you pegged as a reasonable man."

"How did you like my little performance, Jim?" Mandy asked. "Wasn't I properly outraged and upset and crying and everything?"

"In drama class I'd give you a failing grade," Jim said.

"Sweetheart, I thought you were just great," Martindale said. Then he turned to Jim. "Now, Mr. Steel and I would like some of that good wine, the special shelf. See if you can find us a good bottle and a couple of glasses.

She sighed. "All right, Daddy. But you don't discuss any important business until I get back. I want to know everything that's going on."

Mandy stood, smiled at Jim, then turned and scampered to the far door that led farther inside the building.

Harvey chuckled and shook his head. "That one is almost too much for me to keep up with. Sure in tarnation she should have been a boy. But she's got a good business head. Knows as much about the business end of mining as I do, almost. And she's only been working at it since her ma died two years ago."

"Yes, she certainly is different. Now, Mr. Martindale, what about this job you need to get done? I'm no hired gun to wipe out some gent you don't like."

"No, no. Nothing like that. Jim, I just wanted you to know that I'm powerful sorry for this indirect way to get you out here. But your bankers promised me that it was the only way that might have a chance of working. They tell me how independent you are, taking on jobs you want to, when you want to. I'm a desperate man, so I sent my daughter to do a man's job and check you out."

He looked up and smiled. "I really do want your help. I had my people in Denver investigate you. They sent me a file an inch thick full of reports and I liked what I saw. So I told them to work out some plan to get you moving out here."

He paused and watched Jim closely. The rawboned, sunburned man nodded but said nothing.

"My trouble isn't on the mining end, or the engineering. That's all fairly routine by now. I've got a bigger problem. It's security."

"I'm no lawman, Mr. Martindale. My file must have proved that."

Mandy rushed back into the room, a bottle on a silver tray and three stemware wine glasses all jiggling. One glass teetered and Jim caught it as it fell.

"Oh, thank the Lord, Jim! Dad would have skinned me alive if that had broken. They were Mama's favorites." She flashed him a double-dimple smile and worked the cork out of the wine bottle, then splashed a sample of the wine into a glass and handed it to her father. He tested its bouquet, held it up to the light to see the color, then sipped it. He nodded.

"Yes, a good one. You may pour." He turned back to Jim. "As I was saying, Jim, it's security. You've worked with the transportation of gold a time or two. That's my problem. Once I get the ingots all poured I have to deliver them to the mint in Denver. That's the rub. I know almost for certain now that I've got an internal spy. Somebody is telling others what I'm shipping and how it's traveling. I set up a dummy load a month ago, and didn't keep it quiet. Then at night Mandy and I slipped in and exchanged the gold bars for lead. The fortified wagon was attacked the next day and we lost one man dead and my boys killed two of the attackers, but they carried off their dead so we never got a clue who they were."

Mandy had poured the wine and handed a glass first to Jim, then her father. She took one herself and sat on the edge of the chair. Jim sipped the wine, and found it delightful.

"Now, I'm back where I began, with a spy, and a big shipment due out of here in just a little over two weeks."

"To Denver?"

"Yes. To Sacramento by armored wagon, then on the train. They're sending a special car with a large safe in it to hold the gold bars. Then it still has almost twelve hundred miles to travel before it gets to Denver. That's one hell of a long way. A lot can happen in that span if the word gets out that there's a big gold shipment. I want you to plug the leak in my security before then, and after that ride shotgun guard on that gold stack right into the mint in Denver."

"How big a shipment is it?" Jim asked. He picked up the wine glass and sipped.

"Not even you will know that. Let's just say it's big enough to be worth the trouble for a gang of desperados to hire twenty or thirty men with extra guns to bushwack a train full of cavalry. Interested in the job?"

"What's the matter with Pinkertons? Isn't this the kind of job they take, detective work?"

"We tried a Pinkerton man last year on something else. He was from Chicago, spotted the first day he arrived. He got beat up that night and crawled on the stage to get out of here the next morning. No, we need a man who will fit in, who looks at home here, who can knock a few heads if he has to, and who can use a sixgun."

Mandy eyed Jim over her wine glass, her eyes sparkling with excitement. "Of course Jim, if you're afraid to take the job . . ." Her voice was too sweet, derisive, baiting him. He didn't even look her way.

"For a job like that I'd have to have an entirely free hand to hire or fire whoever I wanted to. I'd need your backing all the way and some kind of a supervisor's title here at the mine."

"You've got it."

"And I'd want $5,000 when the gold is at the mint as my salary."

A shrill laugh echoed in the big hall. "Jim, you must be joking," Mandy said when she stopped laughing. "That's about ten times too much."

Mr. Martindale nodded. "That's a lot of money for a month's work, Mr. Steel. But if you get the gold there on time, or at least near the time, intact and get it signed off for me, I'll pay you the five thousand, and give you a five thousand bonus, in gold!"

"Daddy!"

"Hush, girl, I know what I'm doing. Have some more wine."

"How big is the shipment?" Jim asked.

Martindale stood and puffed on his cigar. He paced to the window, then came back. "I don't want this to get around. We'll use two different crews to load so nobody knows how much we put on board the wagon. You and I will make a final tally. I'm sending out a half million dollar's worth in that one shipment."

"That's a lot of eggs," Jim said.

"Yes, that's why I want you to carry the basket."

"Suppose I trip and fall and somehow all the eggs in your basket turn up broken and in Mexico City with me?"

Martindale took a swallow of his wine which he carried on his walk. He looked down at Jim, puffed on his cheroot and blew a perfect smoke ring, then put the end of the smoke through the hole.

"In that case, Mr. Steel, I'd get on a train myself, come to Mexico City and blow your brains out."

Jim nodded. "Sounds fair." He thought about the proposal for a moment. "The only trouble is I've got this deal in Silver City that just can't wait."

"It can wait. I know about that, too, and

you don't have the capital or the borrowing power you need to swing it. You need fifty thousand in cash for the down payment, and a credit total of a hundred and fifty thousand. You won't have it, and can't get it. The mine is the El Toro, and it hasn't really proved out yet. You'd be buying a lick and a promise, on which you could get rich, or which might take you ten years of grubbing to get your money back on a marginal silver ore. Last week the sale price dropped by twenty thousand, but it's still out of your reach."

Martindale drank the rest of his wine and held the glass out to his daughter for a refill.

"Now, Mr. Steel, shall we both quit smoking the Chinese dream pipe and get back to reality? I'm offering you a job that will pay you $10,000 for a month's work. My shipment is due out in about two weeks. That's not much time, but all we have left. Take it or leave it." He smiled. "Of course, Mr. Steel, if you decide not to work for me, I'll swear out a warrant for you on a charge of attempted rape. Even with a womanizer for a judge you should get at least five years in prison. Here in California we tend to protect our women fiercely."

Jim gave a long sigh, stood and walked to the window. He swirled the last of his wine in the glass, then drank it. He could probably get away from the mine with little trouble, but the man would surely charge him as he had threatened and then there would be a wanted poster on him. He didn't want that. The mine owner had a huge problem, and had gone to a lot of trouble just to get Jim out there to talk, and even tested him.

"Young man, there's another good reason why you should take the job. You're a gold man. Doesn't it interest you even a little just how the varmints have infiltrated my company? How they plan to hijack the gold? Will they wreck the train, kill everyone on board and take the gold at their leisure? Or will they simply steal the baggage car and whisk it away into the night? Maybe they'll blow the safe and toss the gold bars over the side to pre-stationed riders. How would you do it if you were on the other side, Mr. Steel?"

Jim laughed. "You're right, I am interested, and wondering how they will make their move. But if I were planning to go on something like this, I'd want at least two months to lay my plans, Mr. Martindale. I'd say you're safe from me even if I do walk away." He came back from the window and put the wine glass down on the silver tray.

His mind was made up.

"You have me in a very unfortunate position, Mr. Martindale, and you too, Miss Martindale. I have little choice it seems but to cooperate with you. But I have some conditions. If I take the job I must have your complete backing: hiring and firing, whatever. I want no budget on what I can spend, I want to make sure that Miss Martrindale is not on the gold train when it rolls, and instead of ten thousand in gold, I'm asking for fifteen thousand."

Mandy laughed. "Impossible, ridiculous. I was right, you are a monster, a self-righteous, conceited monster."

Harvey Martindale took three steps forward to Jim and held out his hand.

"Excellent! Excellent, Mr. Steel. Then it's settled." They shook hands and both smiled. He turned to his daughter.

"My dear Mandy, you may think you're a good businesswoman. But you have a lot to learn. The first is never to become emotionally entangled with workers or employees. The second is simple economics. On this particular point I would have gone to twenty or twenty-five thousand as a salary to be sure the gold gets through. Think of the alternative, of losing the half million to a band of outlaws. I'm sure Mr. Steel thought of that too. But he was too much of a gentleman to rob me right here in my office."

Mandy Martindale lifted her brows in surprise and anger and marched away, her half empty glass of burgundy firmly in her hand.

Jim laughed softly.

CHAPTER 4

Since Jim had no saddle bags when he left Denver, he brought with him a middle-sized carpet bag with clothes, shaving gear, and a few other necessities. He found that Ambrose Smith had been kind enough to drop the carpet bag off the buggy before he drove back to Sacramento. Now in the second floor rear of the big log building, he had been shown a room that would be his for his stay, and unpacked what little he had in the bag. Jim cleaned and oiled his Ruger .44 sixgun and rubbed neat's foot oil into the heavy leather of the holster and his gunbelt to keep them soft and pliable. He put the bottle of oil away and went down for a family style dinner with the Martindales. Mandy did not come to dinner, complaining of a headache which Jim was sure had been brought on by acute embarrassment.

They ate slabs of roast beef and enjoyed two kinds of bread and four cooked vegetables, and finished with hot apple pie. Harvey Martindale had a plan all worked out.

"Jim, I'm announcing in the morning that you're here as an efficiency expert from Denver. You'll have free rein on the whole operation from pick to pour. That way you can get into everyone's way and have my backing. I'll tell them the reason you're here is so I can cut down the overall production costs in order to raise my profit margin. Then I can give the workers an increase in pay. They'll understand that."

"How will they know who I am?"

"That'll take about an hour. By then every man working underground and topside will know who you are and why you're here. It's always that way with my men. They'll know. We'll give you a red steel hat when you go underground. It's the same kind that I wear."

"Sounds simple enough for a smoke screen. I'll start with a quick tour of the hole, then work through the stamping plant and on downstream. I'll spend about half my time in the finished end of things."

Harvey lit a cigar, and offered one to Jim, who shook his head. "Just don't be too obvious. Whoever it is in there knows everything we decide almost before we do."

"You have a night shift?"

"Nope. One crew gives me enough trouble. No sense our going down below tonight if that's what you're thinking. Instead I thought we might have a poker game and the rest of that wine. No sense in letting it go flat. Don't worry, you won't lose all your money. I allow only penny limit poker in my camp, and no bet over a nickel. You game?"

Jim nodded and Martindale brought out a tin box six inches square that was filled with the coppers. They were mostly older ones, the Indian head pennies minted from 1859 to 1864. It was easy to tell because the one cent pieces made before 1865 were called "heavy" pennies by most people. They were made of a copper-nickel alloy and were twice as thick as the bronze pennies minted after 1864. Martindale gave Jim a handful, stacked an equal number of coins on his side of the table, and they began playing.

It was rugged poker. They played as if each cent piece was worth a thousand dollars. At the end of two hours both men had about the same handful as when they began. Martindale shoved the pennies back in the box and said it was bed time for him.

"Breakfast is at six, Jim. If you aren't up, you go hungry. Rule of the household. I'll be ready to show the underground at eight."

Jim thanked him and went up to his room.

The next morning Jim took the normal tour of the tunnel, dropped down a shaft to the four hundred foot level and saw what he considered to be a well run hard rock mine. The stamping plant came next and then the smelter which he moved through as quickly as he could.

Jim began to get interested when the final pour was made on the pure gold into the bar molds. Each of the gold bars was weighed out precisely to ten pounds, and any hundredth of an ounce would be marked on later. Jim watched the two bars cool in the molds, then saw them taken from the molds and put on a small hand pulled cart.

As Jim watched he remembered the calculations he had made last night. Ten pounds to a bar, or 160 ounces of gold per bar and at $20.70 per ounce, that would be a little over three thousand, three hundred dollars worth. At that price it would take 152 bars of ten pounds each to be worth a half million dollars. Fifteen hundred pounds of gold, and he had to get it safely to Denver. This was going to be so simple he'd die of boredom, or so tough that he might not live to brag about it.

Jim followed the little cart which carried the two bars of gold. As soon as it left the pour room they picked up two armed guards. They carried sawed off shotguns and walked right behind the man pushing the small cart. They went along a concrete walkway between the two big smeltering buildings, down a slight incline to what they called the vault. By this time the gold bars were totally cooled and could be handled with soft white gloves.

The only entrance to the vault was down another ramp, then into a small wooden building against the cliff. Inside the building was another armed guard with another shotgun. The guard at the door looked at the other two guards, then at Jim.

One of the roving guards handed a paper to the door guard who checked it, looked at the two gold bars on the cart and marked the paper, then looked at Jim again.

"This the one they said hired on?" the guard asked.

"Yeah, got to be him," the other one said.

The door guard knocked on the door three times, then moved a big handle and opened the door a crack.

"This is guard one, I have passage for two persons, the cart man and a red hat. Passage for two men only."

A guard from inside the open door repeated the message, then the door swung outward. It was a foot thick on heavy hinges, and what looked to be simple rough lumber on the outside was backed with steel plates, an inner core of rocks and steel plate and wood on the other side. It was an unbreakable sandwich of a door.

Inside the vault it looked like another mine tunnel, and Jim realized they were in a worked-out section of the mine, probably a tunnel that played out quickly.

At once he saw kerosene lamps that lit the inside of the tunnel. The door closed and the guard put down his shotgun and built a smoke. He shook out the tobacco from a cloth pouch and rolled the smoke quickly, licked the paper and pinched off the end and then lit it. Jim watched the smoke and saw it wafting away from the door. There was an air vent somewhere.

"So you're the new man," the guard said.

Jim nodded. "True. How long is this tunnel?"

"About fifty feet. Played out the first week they dug here, then they tried some more holes and hit it big. That's why they use this one for the vault. No other way in or out of this tunnel, and no shafts sunk from it."

The man with the cart waved and they moved on back through the tunnel that was lit with more oil lanterns. Half way to the end they came to a worked out "room" about twenty feet high. Jim stopped and stared at the sight.

The cave-like room was lit by a dozen lanterns. On the floor stood three sturdy tables, and on each of them in neat rows were bars of gold. Jim had never seen so much of the pure yellow before in his life.

Each of the three tables had bars stacked in rigid rows of six and four each. He counted quickly and saw that there were 14 stacks of the bars; that meant 140 bars were already there.

"So this is the place. I'm the richest man in the world. But I never think of it as money, or what it could buy. It's just yellow to me. Gets on my gloves, sometimes on my pants. But it washes out." He grinned through jagged, blackening teeth. "Hell, it's not so hot. You can't eat the stuff. I used to have the greatest job in the world. I worked in a bakery. That was good. I could stay there and eat my way through a loaf of bread or a cake or maybe a dozen cinnamon rolls!"

"Are you in charge here?" Jim asked the small man.

"Hail, no. I'm just the delivery boy. You go on down the road there and you'll find the big shot in his office. His name is Harry, old 'Hurry Up Harry!' " The small man laughed and pulled the cart the other way toward the vault door. The guards waved at Jim and followed the cart back toward the entrance.

Jim continued down the tunnel, saw brighter lights ahead and soon came to a "room," another place that had been mined out. This one was different. It had a plank floor, and walls had been set up against the raw dirt and rocks of the cave. The three sides of the office looked almost like a normal room. It had a desk, a small table and three chairs. There wasn't a finished ceiling.

The man who sat behind the desk was a beanpole, long and tall with a thin face, almost no hair and eyes that seemed to have sunk right back into their sockets. Jim saw that the skin had pulled tightly across the man's face to give him a skull like look. The skull's mouth parted and Jim realized the form was alive after all.

"Yes, what can I do for you?" the man asked.

"I'm Jim Steel, on a project for Mr. Martindale."

"Yes, I heard about you. Well this is the most efficient department in the whole place. No loss, no accidents, no lost time. No lost gold bars . . . damn, we're just about perfect here. There is no way we can be more efficient."

"Let's hope that there is. What's your name?"

"The runt out there probably called me 'Hurry Up Harry,' but my real name is Clemmet Alton. Most everyone calls me Clem."

"How many bars you have in the vault now, Clem?"

"With the two that just came back we have 142."

"Is each bar stamped with the actual ounces and our own production indicator?"

"Yes, sir. Strictly according to federal law."

"What other protection do you have here besides the tunnel, the doors and the guards?"

"First there's a switch on my desk. It's connected with charges of dynamite built into the walls along the tunnel from the door to the safe room. The dynamite is replaced each month so it doesn't go bad. I can set off the charges one at a time, splattering any robbers with shards of rock and nails we have planted in front of the powder charges. Or I can blow the eight charges all at once, blocking the tunnel."

"Sounds good, anything else?"

"See this valve?" Clem pointed to a round wheel on what looked like a six-inch pipe that passed through the room along the floor by the far wall. It was a gate valve.

"With this valve I can flood the gold storage room with water in 45 seconds. First I pull this lever which cuts a cord and lets drop a steel doorway that seals off the vault room itself. Then I open this valve and in 45 seconds the room is flooded to the ceiling with high pressure water from the river. It's piped from half a mile upstream. Anyone in the room would be drowned."

"Impressive. I like that. Where does your responsibility for the gold bars end?"

"When they are signed out and put into the war wagon that takes them to San Francisco or to the train. Once they are signed off they are out of my hands."

"Fine, Clem. I just came by on a briefing this morning. Trying to find out as much about each department as I can. I'll be back later. Thanks for your help. Do I just walk out?"

"As long as you don't take any samples."

Jim watched the man's expression, but couldn't tell if he was joking. The skull-like face was blank, and would probably remain so.

Back at the main door, Jim told the guard he wanted out and they went through the reverse procedure of calling out the number of persons coming out.

Jim checked the door again as it swung open. It was counter balanced someway, and he was sure it was a full foot thick. It would take a military 12-pounder to slam through that door even at close range.

Outside Jim talked with the two guards for a minute, found out no one had ever tried to steal any of the gold out of the vault, and that as long as they had anything to say about it, nobody would. The guards said they both had double-barreled shotguns and had a drill worked out so they could fire and load in sequence and put out one round of double-ought buckshot every fifteen seconds for five minutes if they had to.

Jim moved back to the big log building and tried to assimilate what he had seen that morning. He found the cook in the kitchen and she made him a roast beef sandwich and gave him a bottle of creek-cooled beer. He sat on the front steps thinking. So far he had seen five men who knew in detail about the stored gold bars. And there must be night guards on the same areas. Maybe nine or ten men who knew all the procedures to get into the gold vault. But Jim wasn't worried about anyone stealing the gold from the vault. It would happen outside, either on the wagon or on the train. Probably the train where the supply line was longest and the defenses weakest. Yes it would be on the train, but who was it who passed along the vital information? A guard, the little gold pusher, or the vault boss, Clem?

There must be others. There were guards on the armed wagon, a driver and outriders. He guessed about thirty armed men rode with the wagon, too. There could be as many as fifty men who knew when a shipment was made. Of course that didn't include all the management details about when it was going and where.

He thought about it for an hour sitting on the porch watching the flow of men and workers around the mine. He could clean house. Fire or change jobs for everyone downstream from the final pouring of the bars. Clean them out and put in new men. But how would he know that one of the new people wouldn't be reached like one of the current employees had been. The more Jim thought about the problem, the closer he was to deciding that there would be no chance to keep the gold movement a secret. Even if the crooks didn't know the exact time or direction, all they had to do was put a lookout on the trail leading into Sacramento. There was no way they could disguise that war wagon, not even if it moved at night, and then the gold would be on board a train that was definitely headed in one direction. It was a messy thing to turn a train around in the middle of the mountains.

Jim stood, put on his low-crowned hat, and walked toward the shed where he had been told the war wagon sat. By now he was concentrating more on the defenses he wanted on the train. It looked obvious that the gold was going to get that far. If a date for the shipment had been made, that fact now probably was known to the robbers as well. Still, he would do what he could right here.

Jim went to look at the war wagon. It reminded him of a giant turtle, and he guessed that six horses would pull it just about as fast as a turtle could walk. It was an overland stage coach that had been cut apart and rebuilt with raw metal plates on the sides. The seat had been taken out, the doors pulled off, the roof removed and in their places a box of quarter inch thick steel plates welded into position. Another piece of steel fitted the top and the only access was a trap door through the roof.

Firing slits had been cut in the steel on all four sides. Part of the coachwork remained, but just enough to hold the steel box in place.

The axles were double the size of normal ones for a coach, and the wheels were twice as wide rimmed and the spokes thick as a man's thigh. The front was rigged for a team of six. Jim thought it must be a strange looking rig moving down the valley, but evidently it had served well. He found out that since the war wagon had been used to deliver gold, they had never lost an ounce from it. The gold and the men went in through the trap door in the roof, and came out the same way. Two to four guards sat inside the box checking out the firing slits.

Jim headed back for the office of the mining company. He had to have a long talk with someone about the men, try to pick out any of them who might be unreliable, or bad risks for any reasons.

He spotted Mandy walking ahead of him and hurried so his steps matched hers.

"Hi, in a rush?" he asked.

She looked at him, her face frozen, then she giggled.

"I was, but I'm not. There is no way I can stay angry at you for very long, Jim Steel."

"Good, I hope you weren't mad at me for taking the job. I mean, I did cheat you out of watching a hanging."

She laughed. "Oh, that was all just bluff. Daddy is so soft-hearted he'd never do that, he can't even shoot a horse when it breaks a leg." Her double dimples came back and they both laughed. She was still the prettiest girl he had seen in a dozen campouts and mining camps, to say nothing of all of Denver. He asked her if he could look at the work records of some of the men and she flashed him a smile that said "of course," and led the way into the office. As they went up the broad steps she caught his arm and he had to admit, it was a pleasant feeling. Then they were inside and he was back at work.

CHAPTER 5

The Westerner Saloon was not the best in Sacramento, but it was home to Forest Billings and he was happy to see it after the long train ride from Denver. He went down the alley, unlocked the door to his private entrance, and stepped inside. Billings locked the door again and climbed the steps to his second floor office and apartment. As he went up the stairs he pulled the priest's collar from his neck and took off the plain black vestment. He had bought the priest clothes at the last minute in Denver and had been late for the train because he had trouble figuring how to put it on. But he had made it.

Now he threw the dark clothes to one side of his office and sat in the heat of the summer afternoon. Some days Sacramento could be terrible. He wiped sweat from his forehead, sat down and looked at the notes he had made during the trip. He had to remember as much about the railroad and their procedures as he could.

Billings had no regrets about the two men he had hired to rob the train. They had been on board when the cars left Denver. They both knew the dangers of pulling a gun. They agreed to take that risk for fifty dollars each and whatever loot they could get from the passengers. One of them had the bad luck to go up against Jim Steel's hogsleg. An accident which couldn't be predicted or prevented.

But the action did tell Billings a lot about the man he had taken the train ride to watch. This Jim Steel was at least as good as the stories about him, and that brought a touch of a frown to Forest Billings's face. The man would make the project tremendously more difficult. Now he was sure: Steel should be eliminated somehow before the trip began. In the back of his mind he had hoped that one of the gunmen on the train would have taken care of the matter, but it hadn't turned out that way.

Billings pulled a cord by his desk. The cord rang a bell and raised a flag in the kitchen, and soon Wong would come running up the stairs. Billings was tired, unhappy, and also hungry. The unhappy part was going to be the hardest to take care of.

Wong came in after knocking. He was five feet tall, slender, still had his Chinese pigtail, and could outwork a white man twice-to-hell-on-Sunday.

"Chop chop, Wong. Plenty food me. You Hurry." The Chinese stared at him a moment, turned and ran ten feet to the door. He ran! That's what Billings liked about these Chinese. They were workers. Eventually they would probably own half of Sacramento, but for now, they served his purposes very well. If he ever found a Chinese over six feet tall, he'd hire him as chief bouncer in the saloon.

An hour later, just as it was getting twilight, Billings had eaten, finished a small bottle of local wine, and sent for a man to come see him. When the gentleman arrived he took off his hat and then dusted the chair before he sat down.

"Jennings, I think we've got ourselves some trouble." Billings outlined what he knew about Jim Steel, and how he happened to be in the area. "He's their ace in the hole, I'm afraid. Now we need one. Any ideas?"

The man who sat in the chair was poorly dressed in a frayed suit coat and blue jeans that had been patched a dozen times. The old army boots he wore had been thrown away by someone else. Jennings had a bald

71

pate with a few fringes of gray hair around his ears and neck. Three blackened teeth showed on his upper gums when he grinned. Now he spoke softly.

"It would seem to me, Mr. Billings, sir, that you indeed are in dire straights and that you quite properly have come to me for advice and counsel."

"You are a lawyer, or were, Jennings, before your wine bottle collection grew to such proportions." Billings tossed Jennings an old whiskey bottle filled with wine from the keg downstairs. "See if that will help your sodden memory."

"So you're worried about Jim Steel?" Jennings said. "I saw the man. Not so big, but dangerous looking, and I hear he shoots a mean .44. Guess the stories about him are true. My best advice is to take him out of the picture early on. Get a pair of those Springfield rifles. Not the short carbines the cavalry used, but the long guns. Put two men in the hills around the Lucky Seven and wait until Steel's a good target, and blast away. Make sure on the first two shots. Those Springfields are good from 3,500 yards away if you've got a man who can really shoot one. But you move your man in to about 400 yards or so, maybe a quarter of a mile, and it will be like shooting fish in a bucket."

Forest was nodding before the man was done. He liked it, and the long range idea would make it easier to keep his men safe and unmasked. "Will, at times you are downright brilliant. That will be the number two part of my plan. First we see what happens on the other part. Yes, the Springfield, fine weapon. I think I can find two of them with no trouble, and the .45 amunition for them. Now, any more thoughts about our big project?"

"Sir, I have been wringing out my brain cells on that particularly problematical situation, expending a considerable amount of my valuable time contemplating it."

"Meaning, Jennings, you haven't another idea?"

"The truth of your utterances is undeniable."

"I thought so. Now take your bottle and get out of here."

"My fee sir!" Jennings said, standing, cradling the bottle of wine to his bosom. Billings flipped him a five dollar gold piece which the lawyer caught and tested between his teeth. Then he wandered over to the door where he saluted, fell against the jamb and at last got into the hall. Billings bet himself a dollar the old drunk would fall down the back stairs. He won.

By ten o'clock that night Forest Billings had smoked a cigar, taken a bath, shaved and dressed. Then he went down to the saloon and circulated. It was good for business. He caught a high sign from behind the bar, so headed over. The barkeep poured him a cup of coffee.

"Mr. Billings. I think you're needed in the private room, sir."

Forest took the cup of coffee and sipped it, watched the crowd for a moment and tried to figure out the take at the gambling tables. Then he put the cup down and walked behind the piano to the door that led down a short hallway and into a plush private gambling room where the big stakes games were played.

Forest opened the door quietly and stepped into the room. The lights were subdued except over a fancy six-sided poker table with pockets for chips along the sides and soft chairs. No one sat at the table now. A tall man stood with his back to Forest, but the saloon owner recognized him. He let the man talk for a while in his pleading, whining voice. Then Billings stepped up behind him and hammered his fist hard into the talker's kidney.

The tall man yelled in pain and spun

around, murderous fury on his face, in his sunken eyes.

"Goddamn it who snuck up behind. . . ." He let the words trail off. "Oh, it's you, Mr. Billings."

"Clem, you know I hate it when you start whining that way." He went around and sat down at the poker table and began playing a hand of seven up solitaire. "How much tonight, Clem?"

Clem Alton, the man who kept a million dollars worth of gold bars safe and sound for the Lucky Seven mine was in tears. "I . . . I . . . I don't know, they kept yelling at me. They laughed at me! I guess I lost a couple of hundred or so."

The man Clem had been talking to when Billings opened the door laughed. His name was Art Riverton, and he was a card shark and gambler who could make a deck of cards stand up and dance an Irish jig.

"Two hundred like hell, Clem. I've got your marker for six hundred here, and another one for three hundred more." Art reached in his shirt pocket and took out two more slips of paper. "And here's one for two hundred and then this last one for another three hundred. You signed them and dated them all tonight. That comes to a thousand and four hundred Yankee dollars.

And I want you to pay up, right now!"

"Oh Lordy, Lordy! Art you know I can't the hell pay you that kind of money."

"How much do you make out at the mine, Clem?" Billings asked, his voice steady, calm, almost friendly. Clem leaped at the softer tone.

"Mr. Billings, I told you last week. I make twelve dollars and fifty cents a week. That's fifty dollars a month, and it's steady work."

"Yes, you did tell me that last week, that's when you lost almost a year's pay. I'm going to have to attach fifty percent of your wages out at the Lucky Seven. It's the only thing I can do, Clem."

The man with the sunken eyes and the skull-like face staggered to a chair. "Half my pay? What will I live on? I need that money. You can't do this."

"Now, easy, Clem. Sure I can do it. I've got legal and binding notes from you that say you owe me nearly three thousand dollars. That counts your tabs from last month as well."

"But you said them from last month was all paid for!" Clem shouted, jumping out of the chair. Art pushed him back down.

"Paid? Did I tear up your I.O.U.'s? Did I give them back to you for services rendered?"

"No, but you said if I told you how, you know, the safety things we have set up around the gold. You said . . ." He wiped a hand across his face. "Damnit, Billings, you tricked me."

"And you owe me a hell of a lot of money, Mr. Alton. Would you want me to go to your boss? You think old ramrod-straight Martindale would let you work another day if he knew how often you lose money at cards?"

"Hey, you wouldn't tell him. You promised!"

"True, but you promised to pay me for these I.O.U.'s. If you go back on your promise. . . ."

"But to you it's just more money. It doesn't mean a thing. You've got more money than you can use. To me it's — I got to live!" He tried to stand but Art pushed him down into the chair. The next time he moved Clem pulled his sixgun but before he could fire it, Art kicked the weapon away and it fell, bouncing on the floor but didn't go off.

"I think it's time I had a long talk with you, Clem," Billings said and pulled a chair up near the man. He backhanded Clem across the cheek and reached for the I.O.U.'s from Art. "You see those, Clem? And these others from the last few weeks.

Over three thousand dollars you owe me. You want me to burn up half of them?"

"Oh, God, yes!"

"Then you tell me exactly what I want to know tonight, and I'll burn part of them. Then you tell me what I want to know each time I ask you in the next two or three weeks, and each time you tell me something, I'll burn another one. You can earn back your three thousand dollars that way, in just a couple of weeks. That's as much money as you could earn in six years, Clem."

"You bet I'll do it. No tricks?"

"No tricks, Clem. We're buddies, we've got to help each other, right?"

"Yeah, right, Mr. Billings."

He took out the I.O.U. for six hundred dollars and laid it on the green felt of the table beside a match.

"Now, Clem, we need some answers. How much gold is in the vault right now?"

"You won't tell anybody I done told you?"

"Of course not, Clem. Now how much?"

"A hundred and thirty-eight ten pound bars. When it gets to 152 bars it's worth a half million dollars."

"How many guards inside the war wagon when they take the gold to the train?"

"Two or four. Sometimes three or four,

depending how many Mr. Martindale decides."

"Good, Clem. We're getting somewhere now. Is there any chance that a party of ten men could swarm into the mine at two in the morning and steal the gold from the vault?"

Clem sat there a long time thinking. At last he shook his head. "Nope. Not unless I was inside to help you, and probably not even then. Mr. Martindale has alarms he sets at night and only he knows where they are. Then there's the steel door and the locks, and the dynamite and the flooding valve for the holding room. No, sir. Not without a lot of help, a lot of luck, and at least fifty men, I don't believe you could take the gold from the vault."

"You're convinced of this?"

"Yes, sir. It couldn't be done without capturing the whole mine and the workers, everything."

"What if you were to work on the night guard crew, cut off all the charges, shut off the water flow, even push open the big door? What if you were going to get fifty thousand dollars in gold as your share if we could steal it all? Then do you think it could be done?"

Clem picked his nose and smeared the

mess on his black pants without thinking about what he did. Slowly he shook his head, his eyes twin dots deep in his skull.

"No, sir. Not even with me inside. Mr. Martindale, he's just got too much against you. No way a mortal man gonna rob that vault and live long to tell about it. Them guards got shotgun shells they load themselves. They put in what they call double-ought buck. That's a lead slug about a quarter the size of a .45, and they stuff seven or eight of them in a 12-gauge shotgun shell. You imagine what them seven big chunks of lead do to a man?"

"And the guards use them?"

"Oh, yes sir. I saw one guard blow a jack rabbit half way to San Francisco one day. Not enough left at twenty yards to find more than ears and feet."

The two gamblers went to the far side of the room and talked quietly for a minute. Then they came back.

"Clem, when's the next shipment set to leave the mine?"

"Don't rightly know, Mr. Billings."

Billings grabbed Clem by the throat. "We're not playing games here, Clem. If you know and don't tell us, we'll kill you right where you sit in that chair. You understand?"

The gambler's hand came away and Clem

80

cleared his throat a few times so he could talk.

"Oh, yes sir, I understand. It's just that there ain't been any date set yet. I got to know two days before, so I can pack the gold. And they ain't told me to pack it yet, so it ain't gonna be for two days at least. I got to wrap the gold bars in muslin, then put them into little cardboard boxes. We put four in a box so a man can carry them easy. That way the gold don't get all nicked and battered, and nobody can scrape it with a knife. Nobody told me to pack the gold yet, so nothing is shipping out for two more days."

Art nodded. "Far as I remember that's what the outrider told me the night he got drunk. He's been out there long enough to know. Rides on every run they make."

"Clem, take the match and burn the I.O.U. Only not on the table, do it on the floor."

Clem Alton grabbed the match, almost broke it as he scratched it on the floor and with trembling fingers, burned the offending scrap of paper into ashes, then he stomped the ashes into the wooden floor with a grin of satisfaction.

Before he looked up a sixgun muzzle pushed upward hard in the soft flesh under

Clem's jaw, and made him lift his chin to lessen the pain.

"Clem, I'm not going to blow your head off tonight," Billings said. "So you keep your eyes open for me. If you hear anything about a shipment, you let me know that same day. I don't care how, but you ride into town and let me know right away, you understand?"

"Yeah, yeah, I'll do it. Right!"

"Damn right you will, Clem. Where did the last shipment go, Denver or San Francisco?"

"San Francisco."

"Then this one might go to Denver?"

"Might, I just don't know," Clem said.

Billings put the sixgun away and tossed Clem a silver dollar. "Go buy yourself one beer, Clem, and just one, then ride back to the mine. Be sure to buy your beer down the street. I don't ever want to see you in the front part of my saloon again, understand? From now on you come to the back door and knock. Somebody will let you in the back. Now, what are you going to do?"

"Go get a beer."

"And after that?"

"Watch and see when the next shipment is going out. Then come tell you as soon as I can."

"Right, Clem and then we burn the rest of your I.O.U.'s."

Art hustled Clem out the back door, and the two gamblers stared down at the green felt table cover.

"I thought you were sure the next shipment would go to Denver," Art said.

"I think it will. Why else would Missy Martindale go all the way to Denver and check out this clown, Jim Steel, and then bring him back here? He knows Denver. Probably knows the railroad too. At least I've been over the line once now. We still have a lot of work to do." He went to the bar at the side of the room and poured himself a drink. "Speaking of Missy Martindale, how is that part of our plan coming along?"

Art snorted. "Everything right on schedule. That's one little project I'm going to enjoy. It's all set for day after tomorrow when she takes her morning ride on that fancy palomino horse of hers."

"Everything is ready?"

"You bet, and especially me. She's one sweetheart I intend to see a lot more of."

"You touch her Art, and I'll blow your head off. She's a commodity, not a toy. She's a valuable property if she's in one piece and unmolested, you understand.

We've got all the doxies around here you can handle."

"Yeah, okay, you never worried about that part before."

"I'm worrying now. If she gets raped while she's gone old Martindale would drop everything else and come after us with all the guns and brains and money he has. Just make damn sure she can't identify anyone or anything. Make absolutely sure of that."

CHAPTER 6

The second morning Jim was at the mine, he had breakfast with the others at the big kitchen table near a large Franklin stove that glowed with welcome heat. He sat on the oven door for a minute before the cook chased him off, then bellied up to a working man's breakfast: orange juice, a sixhigh stack of hotcakes with three sunnyside eggs on top, a big pitcher of maple syrup, fresh butter, and a plate half full of sausages. Jim ate it all, had two cups of coffee and watched Mandy at the other end of the table stowing away nearly as much. This morning she wore a brown corduroy divided skirt and boots, and carried a short leather crop. After breakfast she put on a jockey style red cap and turned around for Jim's inspection.

"Do I look like a proper lady to go riding this morning?" she asked, her double dimples breaking through.

" 'Pears as how. But I don't think those

proper Boston ladies get anywhere near a horse, especially a quarter horse which you'll probably be riding."

"Not at all, Mr. Steel. I'll be on Lady, my palomino. She's the prettiest horse I've ever seen."

"Well, just don't get lost," Jim said.

"Lost? You are joking now. I've ridden every morning through these hills for the past six or seven years. You couldn't get me lost out there blindfolded at midnight." She waved at him and ran toward the downstream side of the mining operation where the company stables were located.

Jim watched her go, then headed for the war wagon. He wanted to check it out again. Something bothered him about it, but he hadn't quite figured out what. Maybe it was just the idea of someone being penned up inside that steel box with people shooting at him from the outside.

An hour later, Jim came up from the first level of the mine after a token visit, and saw a man riding in hard jump off his mount and run into the mine office. Jim walked that way and a moment later Harvey Martindale came out buckling on a pair of six-guns. He saw Jim and waved him over.

"Look at this note. Some drunk gave it to a rider who was headed this way." He handed Jim the piece of paper.

The note was printed in crude, block letters but the meaning was clear:

"Mandy Martindale is kidnapped. We demand $20,000 in gold. Pick up instructions where to take the gold and find the girl. They are at the lightning scarred oak tree at the bend in the creek a mile downstream from your mine."

"Get your horse, Jim. Let's get down there and see if we can spot Mandy anywhere. This might be a false alarm."

Jim saw that Martindale was tight-lipped and pale and his hands unsteady. They mounted and rode out too fast, so Jim held up his hand and slowed the horses, letting them trot for a quarter of a mile.

"I've been afraid of something like this for two years now," Martindale said. "Ever since she got big enough to ride alone. She didn't want a guard going along with her. I explained that she wasn't as safe as other girls. I told her this might happen. She laughed at me."

"We'll find her, get her back safe and sound, Mr. Martindale. This could be some part of a plot against you and the mine as well, remember that. You can't let this make any difference in your security, in your operation here. It could be exactly what the kidnappers want. It might be tied in with the try for the gold shipment."

"I hadn't thought about that."

They rode awhile in silence, then they saw the bend in the creek ahead and galloped to it. The message was held to the tree by a knife. Jim pulled the knife out and handed the folded paper to Mr. Martindale. He read it and gave it to Jim:

"If you want to see your daughter alive again, bring $20,000 in gold bars to Round Top Mountain Valley, at 11 A.M. today. Half way up the valley there's an abandoned ranch house. One man must bring the gold in an open wagon pulled by one horse. The man is to bring no gun. The light wagon is to be left at the old ranch house and the driver must walk back down the road. The gold must be in the wagon in plain sight. After it is inspected and tested, the girl will be brought up and released."

Jim read the directions again. "Let's get back to the mine, we don't have much time to make our plans."

At the mine, Jim had Martindale pick out

the ten best rifle shots from his guards and workers and armed them. He also took two guards with their shotguns and double-ought buck.

"We'll send the gold?" Jim asked Martindale.

"Absolutely! No fake, no lead gold-plated. I won't risk the life of my little girl that way." He ordered six bars of gold pulled from the storage room and brought to the office. It came in five minutes along with two shotgun guards. He signed the receipt for the order. The wagon and the one horse were made ready. It was a light rig that one horse could pull easily. The gold was laid on a blanket in the box of the wagon so it wouldn't bounce around. It was a good hour's drive to the old ranch house near Round Top.

"You drive it, Jim," Martindale said.

Jim shook his head. "Mr. Martindale, I want mobility. And a good horse and a rifle with forty rounds. We can't know for sure where they will want to make the transfer. Otherwise we could set up an ambush at the ranch house. They're probably already there by now. So we'll have to play it loose. What I figure on doing is to shadow the wagon with outriders on both sides, maybe half a mile away, or closer if we have the cover."

Harvey Martindale sat in a chair in his office, deeply affected now by the suddenness of the crime. "All right, Jim, if you think that'll be best. But I don't want any action taken against those men until we have Mandy safe and sound. Her life is worth a dozen loads of gold like that one. I want you all to remember that." He turned to Jim. "I'll leave the rest in your hands."

"Fine. And I want to be sure you stay here. I don't want them kidnapping you in the process of our getting Mandy back."

Jim pulled his small army together in the big front room of the log building. He told them the main objective was to get Mandy back safe and sound. Only then would they try to recover the gold. He assigned five men to go on each side of the wagon, and told them to stay out of sight at all times. He told one pair of men to be half a mile ahead of the wagon, two more a quarter of a mile ahead, two even with it and the other two sets were spread out a quarter of a mile behind each other.

"We have to remember to be ready to move in any direction at any time. I don't think they'll let us get all the way to the ranch house. The transfer might be any place. After the switch is made, I'll signal with one shot to attack the kidnappers. And if anybody shoots first I'll break both his arms and legs."

It was ten o'clock when they started. Jim figured there were some eyes in the woods around them watching. That was why he held the meeting with the men inside. When they left they went out one at a time, and wandered down to the stables which were in the timber. The men mounted and rode to their assigned points in the cover of the pines and live oak. From there on they would have to use their own judgment about cover. Each man had a rifle and ammunition.

Jim rode to the right of the wagon, staying as close to it in the cover as he could, and just ahead of the rifleman on that side. Jim carried a .56-caliber Spencer sevenshot, with copper cartridges. Not his favorite piece, but it was the best Martindale had left. He hoped he would get up for some closer work.

The wagon moved at a fast walk for the first four miles down the valley, then turned to the right up another valley, and far ahead Jim could see a burned out barn and a decrepit wooden frame house. He stared out across the valley through an occasional opening, but couln't see any of the hidden riders. That was good. He moved a little ahead of the wagon now and looked back down the valley. Nothing. He could see no sign of the kidnappers. Jim was starting to get worried. He had expected the contact to be made before now. They were half way up the valley. If they got all the way to the house, it would provide ideal fortification for the kidnappers' squad of riflemen. Jim didn't want any shooting at all until Mandy was well in their control and out of range.

When the exchange was made, he would wait for some time before he gave the order to attack the others. Mandy's safety was the most important element. He really didn't care if they got away with the gold, but he would like to capture one of them alive, to find out who put them up to the kidnapping.

Jim had assigned the men closest to Mandy when she was exchanged to ride out and get her, and take her away from the place as fast as possible. One man would ride double with her, and the other serve as rear guard.

The wagon moved on, another quarter of a mile and came to a crossing of the small creek. The horse paused and reached down for a drink.

A rifle shot snapped in the stillness of the valley, and the horse stopped drinking. Jim worked his horse closer to the edge of the cover, more pine and live oaks, that ended fifty yards from the wagon.

Then they waited. There was no movement for five minutes, and Jim wondered for a moment if the kidnappers had really fired the shot. Then a voice stabbed from the brush nearest to the wagon.

"Driver, get down and walk home," a voice commanded.

The driver had been instructed to do whatever he was told, and now he stepped from the wagon and walked back the way he had come. When he was out of pistol range, a man darted from the brush on the far side, ran the thirty yards to the wagon and checked the gold bars. He cut each one with a knife to make sure it wasn't lead or gold-plated lead. When he was sure, the man held his rifle over his head and waved it back and forth. From behind the burned out shell of the barn, a black buggy with side curtains wheeled out and drove quickly the quarter of a mile to the wagon. The buggy stopped, hands reached out and took the gold bars as they were handed into the buggy. Then Mandy was helped from the carriage. She was dressed the same as at breakfast even to holding the riding crop. She stood there quietly, listening to the men talking.

A knife flashed in the midday sun, but Jim saw that it was being used only to cut the wagon horse from the harness. The man who had stopped the wagon swung up on the horse and rode hard into the woods heading almost directly for Jim. The unseen man in the buggy whipped the horse and tore down the valley road toward the opening at the far end on the way back to Sacramento. Jim waited until the horse had moved two hundred yards away from Mandy, then he leveled his Spencer and fired at the fleeing buggy. The big slug went to the left, but it brought a volley of shots from the men on both sides of the valley.

Jim turned his rifle toward the rider coming toward him. He lifted it to fire when another rifle snapped to his left and the horse stumbled and went down. The kidnapper fired two pistol shots in the direction from which the round had come, leaped off the dying horse, and dove behind some rocks.

Jim could see his legs, and put one round into the area. The man leaped to his feet and started to run further into the woods when two rifles cracked almost at once. The man threw up his rifle turned around in the air once like a floppy-armed doll and then crumpled to the ground. Jim knew he was dead.

Now Jim spurred his horse toward the fleeing buggy. He motioned for one of the other riders who broke from the brush about the time he did to stay with Mandy. Then Jim rode hard. Ahead he could hear the running fire fight. Shooting off horseback with a rifle is usually as effective as throwing rocks. Three men had converged on the buggy from each side, and now the buggy was as far down valley as the last of his riflemen. Jim saw one man stop his horse, level out his long Springfield rifle and fire a shot. The black horse pulling the buggy seemed to dissolve. Its front legs hit the dirt on their hooves, then folded and crumpled into the dirt, throwing the horse forward in the traces. The buggy lurched forward suddenly, careened to one side and then flipped over suddenly as the leathers of the harness stopped it.

Somehow the man inside came out of the turned over buggy firing two sixguns.

"Take him alive!" Jim shouted, but he was too far away. "Cease firing!" Jim shouted again. One of the close by men heard him, but the men across the valley couldn't, and they quickly stopped their horses and traded shots with the gunman who had dropped behind some scrub growth to hide. Six rifle shots went into the brush and for a moment the man screamed, stood upright and fired both pistols only to be cut down by another volley of rifle fire. He crumpled and lay still.

By the time Jim got to the spot the kidnapper's pistols had been kicked away.

"Who put you up to this fool's errand?" Jim asked the man.

"Water?" the man asked. They didn't have any. One of the men ran to the stream for a hat full.

"Who hired you?" Jim asked again.

The man laughed, lifted one of the gold bars, and died as he smiled at it.

Jim mounted, and rode back to where Mandy still sat on the wagon. A rider stood nearby trying to talk to her.

"I was stupid, stupid, stupid!" Mandy said as Jim rode up. "Daddy told me to be careful, that this might happen. Did anybody get hurt?" She looked at Jim with a sense of relief, as the tears streamed down her cheeks. Her eyes grew puffy and red and she rubbed them.

"Was anybody hurt?" she asked again.

"Yes, Mandy, the two kidnappers are dead."

The shock of it stopped her crying. She stared at him, her eyes vacant for a moment, then the tears and sobbing came again.

"Get on in back of me," Jim said firmly, riding up next to the wagon. She didn't move. "Mandy, get on this horse!" He said it sharply and she nodded, pushed her leg across the broad brown back of the animal and sat behind the saddle. Then she put her arms around Jim's chest and hung on. Her face went hard against his back and he felt her tears wetting him through to the skin.

They rode up where the men had tied the two dead men over the backs of horses. To one side a pistol shot sounded where a horse had been screaming, then it was silent. The only other sound for a moment was the sobs coming from Mandy Martindale. Jim gave the old army "forward" signal and they rode back to the Lucky Seven.

None of the mine workers knew either of the dead men. One of the guards had found the rest of the gold bars scattered among the wreckage. Jim told him to bring it back to Mr. Martindale. The guard grinned, looped the handles of the carpet bag over his saddle horn and turned into the line of march.

It was a sober group that rode toward the mine. None of the thirteen men had been injured, not even nicked by the flying lead.

Jim didn't know what the others were thinking of, but he was having trouble believing it ever happened. The kidnappers had made no efforts to hide their faces, which meant they were inexperienced or figured they wouldn't be around long enough to be identified. On top of that they had ridden themselves into a trap. The narrow valley was exactly the wrong place to make an exchange of money for the victim. The man driving the buggy had only one direction to go to get away. He had to drive downstream, into the rest of the attacking force. The one man with the horse had the right idea, head for the tall timber and keep going. Unfortunately he rode right into three armed men.

Trying to run the buggy straight down the valley looked like a stupid move, unless that's what these hired men had been told to do. Hired men? They were strangers, didn't expect to be identified, here today, gone to Texas tomorrow. Or was that what the people who hired them wanted them to do . . . wanted them to die. Even if they were caught and wounded they could talk, could tell who hired them and where. But dead men can't talk.

It was almost an hour before they came

within sight of the mine buildings and Jim saw four horses ride out from the stables, running fast. Harvey Martindale met them a half mile below the mine. He had three men with rifles riding with him. He spurred forward eagerly when he saw Mandy. She almost fell off the horse hugging her father. Then she jumped off, and Martindale got down and caught her hand, then put his arms around her and they walked back to the mine.

The escort of seventeen horsemen walked with them, surrounding the pair in a reflexive and protective move.

A half hour back at the mine office Harvey Martindale gave two double eagles to each of the men who had gone on the strike against the kidnappers. They were all on the porch, tipping cold bottles of beer he had ordered for them.

"Men, I'm thankful for the way you went out there to help me. It's no fun being shot at, and both Mandy and I appreciate your help. I'm just thankful to God that we were successful. I am sorry that those two men died, but violent men often die violent deaths. I'll send them into town tomorrow on a wagon. See if anybody knew them."

An hour later the men were back at their regular jobs in the mine and the kidnapping was history.

Jim, Mandy, and her father sat around the dining room table sipping champagne in celebration.

"Daddy, I promise never to ride anywhere alone again. I'll always have a friend or one of the guards with me, I promise, I'm just sorry I caused you so much trouble."

Harvey Martindale smiled. "It was no trouble at all. When I think of all the joy you bring me, a little squib of a bother like this doesn't even register." He wiped his eyes, turned away for a minute, then looked back at them and set down his glass.

"Now enough of this. It's time we got back to work and time for you, young lady, to have a bath and then a nap. Now off you go."

When she had left, Martindale turned to Jim. "All right, now you can tell me. What are you so worried about? It's sticking out all over you like hoarfrost."

"I'm still trying to figure out that kidnapping. It was one of the worst ever planned. It was almost like they wanted to get caught, like they knew it wouldn't work when they were doing it. They made the exchange as you know when we were heading into the valley. It put most of our men in a position to cut off their escape route *down* the valley.

Why would anyone do that on purpose?"

"I don't understand the criminal mind, Jim."

"But from a purely logical standpoint it was idiotic. And why try to make the get-away in a buggy? That was stupid. A horse-man would have a chance through the timber, splitting up, going in opposite directions. But not in a buggy.

"The ony answer I can come up with is that whoever set up this little affair is trying to get at the next gold shipment. If that's true, what kind of monsters are they? They set up their own people to die? And what for? Just to put more pressure on you and your mine so maybe, just maybe it will affect the next shipment? That's a thin kind of logic. Did they hire some trail bums to do the dirty work with a promise of a big payoff? If they're that brutal, heartless and cold, what will they do when they have their sights set on a half million dollars in gold? There will be nothing that they will not try, nothing that will be too terrible, too costly, too animalistic for them to try."

Harvey Martindale shook his head sadly. "Jim, I don't know how to answer you. I see no way that our local law can deal with people like this. Maybe you should go into town and talk with our sheriff. He's a good man. Honest, aboveboard. Mandy asked if she could go on the train with the shipment, but now I'm absolutely going to forbid her to go. I won't go either if that will help."

"It will help," Jim said. He wasn't sure it would help enough. But right now he appreciated every little bit of good news that came his way.

CHAPTER 7

The morning after the kidnapping, Jim rode into town beside the wagon that carried the bodies of the two slain kidnappers. The driver parked the rig in front of the sheriff's office and caused a minor stir among the townsfolk. A dozen or so had crowded around the wagon to look at the two dead men by the time Jim got into the lawman's office.

It was better than some he had seen, not as fancy as others. The sheriff looked competent enough. Jim handed him the letter from Harvey Martindale detailing what had happened, the names of the men on the posse, and denying all knowledge of the identities of the two victims. The sheriff read the letter twice, then held out his hand.

"Name's Flynn, Johnny Flynn. It's not often I have a wagon deliver two dead men on my step. From the letter I understand your name is Jim Steel." The sheriff looked up, probably connecting the name to the reputation. He glance back at the paper. "You were along on the little fracas?"

Jim said that was right and filled the sheriff in on some of the details, including the stupidity of the whole operation.

They walked outside and the sheriff looked at the bodies. By now there were twenty-five people around the wagon. "I might have seen one of them around somewhere, but I wouldn't know his name. We get a lot of drifters through here, and gold miners." The sheriff called out a deputy to go get a couple of old doors so they could lay out the men on the boardwalk.

"We'll spread them out here for the rest of the day and see if anybody comes to claim them. Word travels pretty fast when we got two stiffs laid out."

They went back inside and the sheriff took out two papers and began filling them out as John-A-Nokes, the usual term for an unknown person in a legal document.

"I've never seen such a stupid plan for exchanging money for the victim," Jim said.

Sheriff Flynn nodded. "Does sound pretty dumb. But then I don't find a lot of university professors among the outlaws I meet. Word should get around quickly on this pair. If nobody claims them, the county will bury them by sundown in our new hill graveyard."

"Then you won't need me any more, Sheriff Flynn?"

"Reckon not. I'll send a deputy out to talk to Harvey. He's about the most honest man in the valley, and I don't see no problems. Tell him to keep the kidnap notes and everything."

Jim nodded. "Mr. Martindale said to let you know that he'd have a shipment moving here in a week or so. He'll make the usual arrangements with the Union Pacific, but he wanted you to know the war wagon will be coming."

"Always glad to know." The sheriff paused and watched Jim from dark eyes. "Is Harvey expecting trouble?"

"He always expects trouble moving gold, Sheriff. But there have been some signs this time that might mean more trouble than usual. In fact, I think the kidnapping was part of some kind of a plan. I don't know how it fits in, maybe just harassment, but it ties in somewhere."

"Harvey have any idea who might be involved?"

"He said he didn't. Not the slightest. If he did I'm sure you'd have the names and some charges."

Sheriff Flynn adjusted the sixgun on his hip and sat in the swivel chair by his desk. "Don't see how it could be a try to take the war wagon. You'd need a company of cavalry to capture that thing. So that leaves the train. The steamer gets out of my jurisdiction just real fast, Mr. Steel."

"Unfortunately. Then that leaves me with 1200 miles to worry about."

Sheriff Flynn snapped his fingers and looked up. "I finally thought of it. You're Jim Steel the Gold Man. You always seem to show up where there's lots of gold."

"Not always by choice. What do you know about Ambrose Smith? Is he as sweet and pure as he makes out?"

"Smith? As far as I know. He's one of Harvey's bankers. Never had any trouble with him."

"He's the only person in town I know. What about a long tall priest with a thin face?"

"Not likely. We've got a trio of padres, but they're all short and fat."

"Just an idea. Well, I'll be heading back to the mine. Let us know if you get any connection between these two bodies and anybody here in town, it might just come in handy."

Jim went outside and watched the crowd

around the bodies. A tall man with a gambler's ruffled shirt and fancy cuffs came out of a saloon and walked over to look at the show. He had a thin face and for a moment Jim thought he should know him from somewhere, then decided he was mistaken.

The little group of people around the bodies kept changing, flowing like a slow landslide, clogging up for a moment, then moving on past. A few women gasped in mock horror and rushed past. While Jim watched, no one showed any indication that he knew the men.

The gambler walked by, shrugged and went back to the saloon. Jim thought of getting a drink before he headed back. The Westerner Saloon was the one the gent had vanished into. But Jim decided he should spend a little time learning the trail between town and the mine instead. He swung up on his horse. The wagon driver had instructions to pick up some supplies while he was in town, and had driven away.

Down the street, behind the window of the Westerner Saloon, Forrest Billings let a small frown line relax along his jaw as he saw the man get on his horse and ride. It had been an unfortunate meeting, but there was no way to avoid it when the man came out of the sheriff's office so quickly. Forrest was not sure but he didn't think that Steel recognized him. He looked a far piece from a priest dressed this way. But he'd have to be more careful.

Forrest stared with scorn at the dead men. They had done exactly as they were told, and he was sure they had also plotted to steal the gold bars once they had them. Their greed and stupidity had served his purposes well. And he hadn't lost any of his men, only the two drifters he had found drunk in his saloon two days ago. Nobody would miss them. He went back into the saloon for an early lunch and some planning.

The next three days at the mine were a windfall of activity. Jim beefed up the war wagon putting another firing slot in one side, and designed some heavy steel and blanket shields for the horses. But at last he decided the contraptions would be too heavy. The fourth day he was back from town they went into the final preparations.

The date was set and in two days they would roll. A message was sent to the sheriff, noting the exact time and place the gold would be deliverd to the railroad, and the route the war wagon was coming. It was in a sealed envelope and the sheriff was not to let anyone but himself know the details. Jim sat at the big kitchen table made of varnished and polished redwood planks, the last day before the war wagon left. He sipped at a second cup of coffee and watched Mandy. She had been lingering over coffee with him.

"Sorry about your not going on the train," he said. "It's just too dangerous. That's where they'll try for the gold, I'm sure of that now. And there's no way we can hide a train so they won't know it's coming. We might get out of Sacramento secretly, or get the gold on board surprising them, but all that would do would be to give us a half day's start. They would telegraph ahead and alert their people down the line."

"That's all right, Jim," Mandy said smiling. "I don't think anything will happen on the train anyway. I did want to go at first, but now Daddy says I get to go to school in Denver this fall, so I'll be getting ready for that. Won't it be fabulous living in Denver?"

Jim laughed. "Do you have any idea how cold it gets there in the winter? You'll probably freeze your nose off. You know how high those Rocky Mountains are?"

"Of course. Denver is the 'mile-high' city. They told me that when I was there last week. That's over five thousand feet. But we've got peaks taller than that in the Sierra just ouside of town a way."

"Sure, but you aren't living on top of these peaks." He got up, waved and went out the front door into the warm sunshine. He had been in the vault room most of yesterday, watching the skull-like man loading the gold bars in the pasteboard boxes. He did it with such precision and care that not a single bar was nicked or scraped. Clem was a man who took pride in his work, Jim decided.

It would take thirty-eight of the cartons with four bars each, 152 of the ten pound bars to make up the shipment. Jim guessed there wouldn't be room in the war wagon's box for more than two guards once all the gold was loaded aboard.

Jim saddled a strongly built mare and rode over the nearby route they were probably going to take to town. It was the most direct. They would have outriders, and guards in front and back. It would be suicide for less than a hundred and fifty men to try to take the war wagon. Attackers could stop the wagon easily, just put a marksman in the trees with a long range rifle and kill the horses. But they would still have the problem of fighting off the guards, then opening the steel box.

Jim spotted a rock outcropping about a

mile from the ranch and rode over to check it out. The rocks would offer perfect cover for snipers, and was less than 300 yards to the center of the valley where they would be driving. He made a note to put at least two men in the rocks and have them there ten hours before the trip started.

He paused on a low hill and checked the route again. There was little more he could do out there now. He was ready. He just hoped the rest of his crew were ready, and that any robber force wasn't. He would find out soon enough.

Back at the big log building he went over the arrangements with Harvey Martindale. Mandy stood behind her father's chair watching, listening.

"So we have two men in the box with the gold," Jim said. "Each man has two repeating rifles and four pistols hung on loops on the steel. Then we have fifteen men in front and fifteen in back of the war wagon, each man with a repeating rifle and a sixgun."

"What about outriders?" Mandy asked.

Her father grinned. "Yes, Mandy. Yes, we'll put ten outriders at twenty yard intervals from the wagon on each side. That should sweep up anything that we haven't checked out before."

Jim nodded, then looked at the next piece

of paper. "What about the train itself? How many men are you sending on the train as passengers?"

Martindale frowned. "Passengers?"

"Yes, guards dressed in their Sunday best. Each man with a sixgun and a derringer. I'd suggest ten. And I'll want to know them by sight before we leave. They'll be our emergency troops."

"Well I hadn't thought of that. Yes, I like it. I'll pick out good pistol shots for that assignment."

"Did we get the setup for the baggage car I asked for?" Jim asked.

"Precisely, James. It will be a combination mail and baggage car, with mail clerk. It has the big safe, a Duncan Safe, which has plenty of room for the gold inside and it's welded to the frame of the car. It comes with a combination lock and two key locks. The engineer will have both keys and the conductor wants the combination but I won't let him have it. Only you, Jim, will have that and I want you to memorize it."

"You mean: right to 4, left two turns to 16, then right to the first 47?"

Harvey Martindale laughed and slapped his knee. "Now where in the world did you find that? You been reading my mail again?"

"Afraid not, Mr. Martindale. I heard you

mumbling the figures the other day, so I memorized them along with you, just before you burned the paper that had the combination."

"See, Daddy, I told you Jim Steel was simply wonderful. If anybody can get the gold through, he can."

Jim grinned at the pretty girl.

"Well, you're right, I hope. James, my boy, I do think we're ready. Tomorrow morning is the time. I may just stay up all night. We'll need a full three hours to get the war wagon to the tracks."

"We still going to the downtown station?"

Harvey Martindale chuckled. "For that, my boy, you'll just have to wait and see."

Orders were to get to bed early. Martindale picked ten of the guards to be on the train as well. The word was that the war wagon would pull out promptly at 3 A.M. Anyone not ready to go would be left behind.

Jim slept lightly and with the first clank in the kitchen below he was up and dressed. Breakfast was a big one. He took ten flapjacks, four eggs, four sausage patties, a mess of fried potatoes and three cups of coffee.

Jim scrambled out the front door and saw that his saddle was cinched up tight on the big mare, then swung on board and rode down to watch them hitching up the team of six. He always marveled at the way the drivers could hold those six sets of leather lines. They had three in each hand, laced between gloved fingers, each hand holding lines for three horses on one side.

The team was hitched. They had finished loading the gold into the war wagon at 2:30 A.M. and the guards had been doubled. Then Harvey Martindale came rolling down in a surrey behind a fleet black horse. Mandy sat beside him. She waved at Jim in the moonlight.

"Daddy said I could come and watch the train get off."

Then they were moving. Jim rode around the guards, checking the outriders, and got his horse lathered up after a half hour. He slowed and cooled her down, then kept checking the riders, the point man and the guards. Everything went smoothly.

When they hit the main valley road leading toward Sacramento, they ran into a pair of riders coming their way. The point man took their sixguns and brought the riders back to Jim.

Jim explained it was a gold shipment, and led the two through the guards and out past the rear security, then gave them back their guns. They said they thought they had a range job if they could find the right spread.

After that, nothing unusual happened.

Jim was a little disappointed, but pleased at the same time. They angled toward Sacramento, then when they were about five miles away and it was getting light, they swung to the left along a faint trail. Jim checked with the lead man and he said this was the route Mr. Martindale had given him. They would come out about four miles outside Sacramento at Shotgun Siding. The train would be there at 6:04 for loading the gold, after it left the Sacramento station at its regular 5:50 A.M. time.

That was the surprise Martindale had for him. Jim accepted it. Loading would be much easier to guard out in the middle of nowhere like Shotgun Siding.

The rest of it was routine. The war wagon met no resistance. The gold was loaded into the huge safe as passengers got off the train and gawked. Some guards spread out and tried to look innocuous.

Then it was done, the big door was slammed shut, the combination lock spun, the two big keys turned and given to the conductor who took them to the engineer. Martindale watched the whole process, then initialed the conductor's bill of lading, and the train pulled out.

Jim had sent his ten passenger guards to board at Sacramento. Now he brought on ten more men as plain guards. Two would be on duty in the baggage car. Two more would be in each of the two other passenger cars. Four would be off duty and sleeping. A sergeant of the guard was supposed to keep rotating the men on and off duty so they stayed rested and alert.

Since it was really governmental business, Martindale had requested thirty armed troopers from the Department of California army headquarters. They said they would send ten men who would board in Sacramento and would detrain at Ft. Ruby in Nevada where they would be replaced by ten new troopers. A sergeant would command each detail.

Jim went into the second car and found his ten army troopers, looking more like they were going on a vacation than guard duty. Jim had the sergeant line them up for inspection and he read them the duties of the trip. They were on guard twenty four hours a day until relieved in Nevada. Their sergeant would report directly to Jim who was the train commander. He at once sent two of the soldiers into the baggage car to stand guard, put another soldier on top of each of the passenger and freight cars, and left the rest for relief and back up. The sergeant, a round-bellied oldtimer who had fought in the Civil War, had a knowing look in his eye as he spoke to Jim.

"I'm Sergeant Andy Southdown, sir. You were an officer in the war?"

Jim nodded.

"I could tell. Always can tell. My boys will do whatever we tell them to. They've been bloodied once or twice. This should be good for them."

Jim nodded. "Thanks, Sergeant Southdown. I'll count on you for some expert help. I'll go through you for relaying orders whenever there's time." Jim turned and went to check on his guards.

Jim had put a small satchel on the war wagon when it left the mine, later collected it and pushed it into a seat on the train just ahead of the baggage car. There were two passenger coaches and one freight car loaded with oranges as well as the engine, tender and caboose. It was a short, workable little train, but still hard to hide.

They chugged away from Shotgun Siding getting up speed as they headed for the mountains beyond. Jim checked the passengers in the first coach. If he hadn't known them by sight he would never have been able to tell the company men from the regular passengers. There were about thirty passengers in the first coach. It was the traditional model, with cast iron seat backs and sides, padded with thick, soft brown upholstery. Most of the seat backs would swing from one side to the other, so you could ride heading forward no matter which end of the car had been aimed that way. It was practical and efficient but not especially comfortable.

In the center of the coach stood a potbellied stove and a supply of wood. In winter the stove woud glow red hot and those who sat near it would be overheated while the passengers at the ends of the car froze.

Jim grinned looking down the car. It wasn't perfect, but it beat the hell out of a stagecoach at twenty miles a day. And no bumps and jolts. Yes, sir, the train certainly was the modern way to travel.

Jim sauntered up the aisle looking at the passengers. There were lots of women, about a third of them, he decided. One small head in front of him seemed to be constantly on the move. He walked past and looked back. The black veil was over most of the woman's face. He looked at her eyes, and he exploded in sudden anger.

"You!" he shouted. "You," his finger pointed. "Come out here this minute. I'm going to have a long talk with you."

The woman stood and moved to the aisle where the veil slid down and the twin dimples poked into Mandy Martindale's cheeks.

"Hi, Jim," she said softly, "don't hit me."

CHAPTER 8

Jim stared down at the pert, pretty laughing face of Mandy Martindale. He was angry, but at the same time he admired her spunk. Most women would have preferred to stay miles away from a dangerous trip like this. He scowled and she giggled.

"Mandy, we agreed you weren't to come, remember? I'm going to have to stop the train at the next station and put you off."

"Jim, you can't do that. You know there isn't a stop along here with any kind of a station or even a town. There's no place at all until way up in Nevada somewhere. Anyway, there are ten or twelve other women on board, so it's just as safe here for me as it is for them. You didn't tell them they couldn't come along because of your old gold."

"Does your father know you're here?"

"Of course. Sure, I wouldn't go away without telling Daddy. Well, he probably knows by now. I left a note for him on the surrey seat. He's sure to find it."

"Mandy, I should turn you over my knee and spank you," Jim said his anger cooling.

Mandy smiled. "Oh, I've heard about that. Go right ahead."

"Mandy, you stop that. I said I should send you back. And you know that I should. You'll be the death of your father yet. Since you're here, you stay out of the way and help take care of the women if any shooting starts, which it probably will. You still have that derringer?"

She nodded.

"Don't use it, just duck your head and stay down if anything happens. You promise now."

"I promise," she said with a smile that negated the whole point.

Before he could move she reached up and pecked a kiss on his cheek.

"Yes, Uncle Jim," she said loudly, and half those in the car heard. Jim turned and went back toward the baggage car to start his check on the guards.

He stopped almost at the end of the passenger car. Jim looked at the man sitting next to the window. Again there was that same thin face, and something familiar. Jim loosened his revolver in its holster and leaned on the seat in front of the man and stared at him. The eyes, there was nothing that could hide the hard, cold gaze of those eyes. Only this man wore a full beard.

The eyes were the same as those of the priest on the train from Denver. The priest who got off in Sacramento but did not have a church there. The eyes were also the same Jim had seen in the gambler who looked at the bodies in Sacramento several days ago and who walked into the Westerner Saloon. Jim pushed the back of the seat in front of the man forward so he could sit down across from the piercing eyes. Now the man looked directly at Jim. Steel's sixgun came up and leveled on the surprised man who had been staring out the window. Steel reached over and pulled at the man's beard. He had seen a place that didn't look quite natural. Slowly the spirit gum of a spot of the beard under the man's chin gave way.

"Well, well, well. The priest who isn't a churchman. The gambler from the Westerner Saloon who is now pretending to be someone else. You do have a time making up your mind, don't you?"

The man started to draw a derringer, but Jim rapped his knuckles with the muzzle of his sixgun and the hand stopped.

"Trooper!" Jim called. The nearest army

blue coat trotted up the aisle, his sixgun out and ready.

"Keep him covered while I search him," Jim said.

"What's your name?" Jim asked.

A red-faced man sitting just ahead and watching the whole exchange with glee spoke up.

"Hell, everybody knows him. That's Forrest Billings, the gent who owns the Westerner Saloon back in Sacramento. What's he doing all dolled up with a fake beard?"

Jim found a derringer in Billings's coat pocket, took it as well as the sixgun from the man's holster. Then Jim pulled Billings by the arm.

"Okay, Billings, out this way. We're going to have a business conference up in the next car. And Billings, you make even the slightest try to get away, and I'll put all six of these .45 slugs into your back, you understand me?"

Billings nodded, his eyes furious.

They walked through the car, around the stove and past the double doors and into the next car. It was the coach that had only the soldiers in it. Four of them were sleeping. Two played cards.

Jim pulled the handcuffs from his pocket. Harvey sometimes gave them to his guards on gold shipments. Jim snapped the manacles around one of Billings's wrists and the other one around the cast iron frame of the window seat halfway up the car.

Jim sat across from him and stared hard at the man. "Just what the hell you doing playing priest coming in from Denver and now in disguise on this train?"

Billings snorted but didn't answer.

Jim backhanded him across the mouth and saw blood form on his cut lips. "A little reminder, Billings. I'm the only law on this train. And we ain't gonna stop for almost a full twenty four hours. I can do almost anything I want to with you: slice off your balls, shoot holes in your kneecaps, or just plain beat you to a bloody pulp with the side of my .45 barrel. How do you want it, simple or hard?"

"I don't know what you're talking about," Billings said. "I'm going to Denver to bring back some girls for my saloon. I want some girls who can sing and dance. I don't know anything about anything else."

"Figures. A couple of days with no food or water will help you remember. I've got to check out my security or I'd stay and play games with you. But I'll be back. I used to know this Chiricahua Apache. He had more ways to make a white man talk than I'd ever

124

heard of. He taught me everything he knew. Think about it."

Jim turned and left, motioning to the sergeant. "Andy, I'm leaving that man in your charge. If he gets away it's your ass. You give your men the word. Now, I've got to check out the guards." Jim turned and walked into the next passenger coach, found Mandy staring out the window at the gorge they were working up. He went on by, through the double doors and into the baggage car.

This one was different from others Jim had seen. The safe was built into the car just past center toward the far end. It occupied half the width of the rail car, and extended to the ceiling and was ten feet long. Beyond it was the baggage, a steamer trunk, and some packages heading back East. The near end of the baggage car contained the mail room. A series of metal racks held mail sacks. A bench in front of them was where they dumped out sacks of mail. The clerk stood there sorting the mail into bags for the right states, and in some cases several states' mail went into the same bag.

The two civilian guards sat on the floor playing cards. One of the soldiers slept on a sack of mail. The other bluecoat had pulled a book from his shirt and went on reading. The car had no windows, only solid metal walls, with one double metal door that rolled open on the off safe side. The side door now was double-locked.

The guard on the end door had looked out, made sure it was Jim, then let him in through the locked baggage car door. There was a small window in the heavy metal for identification. Usually no one but railroad personnel was allowed in the mail car.

The postman-baggage clerk's name was Pete Donner.

"Hi, Pete. What's happening?"

"Nothing, Jim. Just the way I like it. I get one more bag of mail done and I can have a nap myself. Nobody's going to get in that door but you, you can be damned sure of that. If I lose anything from this car, I lose my job, your boss made that certain."

"If you hear any shooting, keep buttoned up tight," Jim said. "I don't think anything is going to happen back here, not at first anyway. They'd have to get the train stopped."

They talked awhile. Pete was from Denver and liked the long run to Sacramento. He'd made it four times now since the new section opened. Jim waved and the cavalryman let him out the locked door.

The more Jim thought about what he said the more sure he was. Any trouble would start outside. First they would stop the train somehow. He went between cars and climbed to the roof. Jim talked to the men riding on top, three of them and told them they would be relieved soon, and to keep a look out for riders or Indians or anything that didn't look right.

Jim worked his way along the roof of the swaying car to the next, then went over the tender and yelled at the men in the engine. They saw him and he went on down to the engine cab itself.

He'd met the engineer, Amos Handshoe, before they left.

"What the hell you doing up here?" Handshoe asked.

"Just roaming around."

A man threw two chunks of wood into the boiler and held up a hand. "You the ramrod on this damn cattle drive?"

Jim nodded.

"Good, hear we got a whole piss pot full of gold back there. Sure hope some Jaspers don't try to borrow it. Give us a peck of trouble if they want to try. I'm Josh."

"I think they're going to try, Josh, so watch for them."

Handshoe was a middle-sized man with a

long handlebar mustache, the ends waxed and curled upward. "Hell, I don't know why I volunteered to take this bitch," he said. "Wanted to see California, do something different. Really wanted to pick an orange right off the tree, but ain't many orange trees around Sacramento. Hell I got me one damned feeling that this run I should have stayed home. But I'll get you folks to Denver, along with your damned gold. Just hope the trouble ain't more than we can handle."

Jim grinned and saw that each man had a sixgun handy and there was a repeating Winchester on the side of the cab.

"Hope you boys know how to use them shooting irons."

The fireman nodded "I done shot that piece oncet or twicet."

Then Josh threw in two more chunks of the two foot long cord wood from the tender. He would be out of wood long before Denver. That meant a stop somewhere down the line. Most of the fuel was split oak, which made for the hottest fire. Jim waved at the men and went back over the tender toward the freight car, and then down to the first passenger coach.

It was just past noon when he slipped into the seat beside Mandy Martindale.

"It's just about time you got here for lunch," Mandy said. She had cold fried chicken, potato salad, two kinds of sandwiches and small bottles of beer. Most of the passengers had opened baskets and were eating. This run was not busy enough yet to justify pulling a dining car, Jim had found.

Jim ate and thanked her. He turned to her. "Now what is this 'Uncle Jim' routine all about?"

She grinned and the dimples dimpled. "That way I can kiss you right out in public and it looks all fitting and proper." She reached up and kissed his cheek again as Jim got up.

Jim started toward the baggage car. The train jolted as the power cut back, and they jerked again as the brakes went on. Steel skidded on raw steel and the wheels of the engine came to an abrupt halt. Sparks flew.

Jim struggled to the passenger car door and jumped outside, then peered out between the cars looking forward. They were on a slight curve, going down an incline and Jim saw the problem. Directly ahead on the tracks maybe a quarter of a mile away was a log. Even from that distance it looked huge and it didn't lie across the tracks, it was lengthways between the tracks. The cow-catcher would have no chance to push the log out of the way. They had to stop.

The attackers had won the first move, they had the train stopped. Before it came to a halt, Jim jumped to the ground beside the tracks and ran ahead to the engine. He got there as they came to a stop and stepped up into the train cab.

"How the hell did that happen?" Jim asked Engineer Handshoe.

"Somebody went to a lot of hard work to get it there. See how the branches have been cut off smooth so they could roll it? We got ourselves some trouble."

"Can't push it off?"

"Not hardly. Just shove it down the tracks, probably tear out a tie or two and worry the rails."

Josh, the fireman, looked worried. "Somebody's got to go out there and roll that son of a bitch off."

"Yeah, Josh. You," Handshoe said.

"How?" Jim asked.

"Pry poles. Got one here in the cab."

"I'll help," Jim said. Josh brought the pole, a steel bar eight feet long and an inch thick. They ran to the far end of the 30-foot long log, because it was smaller and lighter there. Together they put the pry pole under the edge of the log and both pushed upward on the pry pole. The end of the log skidded six inches.

Before they could try again a rifle shot slammed through the stillness and a bullet whined over their heads. Both Jim and Josh jumped down the right of way. The land was open on the right hand side of the train. To the left it was brush-covered. The gunman had to be in there.

"Stay here, I'll go get some help," Jim said. He ran back to the first passenger car, and jumped on board.

"Okay, troopers, all of you, bring your rifles, as of right now you're infantrymen. Sarge, you keep the baggage car covered. Get inside and wait."

Jim jumped down on the right hand side of the tracks and five troopers came with him, all with repeater rifles and sixty rounds of ammo. He had established that right off.

They ran silently behind the low fill of the roadbed ahead up the tracks. The rifleman couldn't see them. Jim figured he could get behind the gunmen, or flank them. He ran and hoped. It seemed like the summer of sixty-three again and he was wearing the blue uniform with captain's bars on his shoulder directing a column of blue coats through that woods. He moved a hundred yards beyond the log, then he and the five men went across the tracks in a rush without drawing fire. On the other side he spread them out in the woods in a line of skirmishers, five yards apart, walking toward the supposed point of gunfire, and making as little noise as possible.

They had moved about fifty yards when one of the men held up his hand and all stopped. Jim moved silently through the brush to the man who pointed to his right. Down a slight slope on the crest of a small ridge lay four men with rifles. As they watched, the men below began shooting at the train, at the windows.

Jim moved the other men up and told them to fire when ready. The first volley thundered through the trees. Two of the ambushers below rolled over dead. Another looked behind him in surprise, then took a round through the head and flopped to the ground. The last man dove for cover and rolled into a small ravine that covered him from the gunmen above.

Jim waved his men out again, spread as before sweeping toward the train. Gunfire erupted almost directly in front of them, and they could hear train windows breaking. Jim spotted them this time, less than fifty yards from the train, gunning at anything that moved.

Jim and two others opened up at once with rifles, and two of the three men below took hits and dragged themselves into the heavy brush.

Jim sent another five volleys of fire into the woods. The men vanished. Two minutes later a horseman appeared for a moment on the skyline of a ridge three hundred yards away, then vanished.

"That's it, men," he said. "Good work. Now let's go over to that log and see what we can do with it."

The men moved at a trot behind Jim and came to the tracks and down to where the engineer and fireman were struggling with two iron pry poles.

"Some fresh muscle," Jim said. The men gave up the pries and stood back giving directions. Every inch they moved the smaller end of the log toward the left rail, moved the heavy butt of the log toward the right rail. They weren't rolling it, simply prying it around in a circle.

"Good, good," Engineer Handshoe said. "If we get it around another two feet we can get the small end over the edge of the tracks, then the cowcatcher will work."

It took them fifteen minutes more of hard, sweating work to get the small end of the log pried onto the rail, then the engineer ran for the train. He brought the engine up and nudged the log, pushed it again, and smoothly the butt end of the log rolled up on the right hand ribbon of steel track. The train kept pushing it and the heavier end pulled the whole log toward the right side of the tracks as it rolled. After about twenty yards, the big log overbalanced to the right and rolled off the tracks and into a small canyon.

A shout of approval went up from half of the passengers who had left the train and had been watching the progress. Now they hurried back on board the train. The attack force had suffered no casualties. Jim looked inside the passenger cars and was surprised.

Half the windows had been shot out, or had gaping holes. No one had been hurt in the baggage compartment. Flying glass had injured two troopers, but they were all patched up.

Inside the passenger car three civilians were hurt. One woman was cut by flying glass, but the blood had stopped gushing and a bandage covered her arm and side.

An elderly man had jumped in the excitement and fallen, breaking his leg. A man bent over him now, and Jim remembered that Martindale had suggested sending along a doctor on the train in case there were some problems. That must be the doctor.

Then Jim saw a third woman hurt. Blood streaked her face. A guard held the woman's head and worked on the blood flow. Then she turned and looked at Jim, and he saw it was Mandy. Jim ran to her and fell on his knees beside her. She opened her eyes, smiled at him, and then fainted.

CHAPTER 9

"Sir, are you the doctor?" Jim thundered, his voice snaking out like a bull whip. A man in the aisle had been wrapping the old man's broken leg. Dr. Reginald Carter did not have to ask if he were needed. He stood at once and took his small black bag with him, rushing down the train aisle, past the cold heating stove to the girl lying on the seat. He was a small intense man with strong hands, a short haircut, and spectacles.

Dr. Carter knelt beside Mandy and touched the pulse at her throat, nodded, and looked at the bloody face. Gently he wiped the blood from Mandy's head with a wet cloth. He found no serious wounds. High in the hairline he discovered two cuts, neither one deep, but both bleeding heavily. He wiped the cuts with the wet cloth, parted her hair and applied some liquid to the wounds, and stopped the blood. Then he covered each wound with a white gauze bandage and taped it in place.

Only then did he look up at Jim Steel. "That should do it. Her pulse is strong, a little fast, but that will go down. She looks healthy and should be fine in an hour or so. These head lacerations always bleed profusely and it looks like serious trouble. But the cuts are minor, nothing to worry about. Get her sitting up, that will help."

Jim picked up Mandy and sat her in the seat and as he did, Mandy revived. She pushed against him for a moment, then opened her eyes and saw Jim and relaxed, mumbled something and smiled. The woman who had helped Mandy before now sat beside her.

Jim held out his hand to the medic. "Doc, thanks," Jim said. "I didn't mean to roar at you that way, I guess I was a little upset."

Doctor Carter smiled. "We all would be more upset if those bandits had broken in here and killed everyone. We all owe you our thanks, Mr. Steel. Not the other way. Now, I'll finish with Mr. Thompson back there. I've put on a splint but it needs some more wrappings. The rest of your people seem to be in good condition." He smiled, turned and walked away.

Jim watched Mandy for a few moments.

She was looking up at him and smiling.

"I'm sorry I bled so much. I don't know why I fainted. I'm usually not that much of a sissy."

"You were hurt, but you'll be fine now." Jim bent and kissed her cheek. "Now you sit right here and rest up, I may need you later to lead a charge or something."

"Thanks, Uncle Jim," she said and grinned. He watched and the dimples came.

Jim walked forward to the next car where the soldiers were quartered. As soon as he stepped into the coach he knew something was wrong. Two of the men in army blue and high boots stared at him and then looked away. The sergeant was still in the baggage car. Jim looked at the troopers wondering what the problem was. Then he glanced at the middle of the car and he knew at once.

The gambler had escaped.

The empty handcuffs dangled from the iron top of the seat back, and Forrest Billings was nowhere in sight.

One trooper came forward. His blue sleeve showed where corporal stripes had been removed.

"Sir, he was gone when we came back from that little patrol with you. He was just gone. When you yelled at us to come help you we all went. We left that joker without a guard and he must have slipped out of the steel bracelet somehow. He was a thin critter as I remember."

Jim swore. He knew he should have thrown the gambler off the train the minute he found him. Then there wouldn't have been this worry about him. Now Billings was loose and had either left the train when it stopped for the log, or was hiding somewhere on board.

Jim waved at the ex-noncom. "Corporal, don't worry about it. He's gone and it's my fault. Get three men and relieve the guards on the top of the cars. Post them yourself. I'm going to check on the sergeant in the baggage car."

Jim hurried back to the gold car, got admitted and looked over the group.

"We're all fine here, Jim," Sgt. Southdown said. "That was quite a little battle you had."

"Don't fret, Southdown, you'll get a turn during the next one. I just changed the rooftop guards. You better get back up front and move your other men around. Bring two new ones in here. These Jaspers have been sleeping too much."

Jim talked to his civilian guards, told them to go out in the first car and pick a broken window and get ready to do some shooting.

"I'm sure those high-graders aren't done with us yet," Jim said. "They'll be back, or some of their bunch will meet us. I want everyone to keep a sharp eye out for that gambler from Sacramento. Tall, thin face, intense eyes. Either he got off the train or he's hiding somewhere. He slipped out of those handcuffs during our little shootout. If he's on the train, let's find him."

Pete Donner threw another letter into a mail sack and scoffed.

"Hell, man. Your gambler or them bandits no-way they gonna get in here. We're safe as on our old mother's lap."

"I hope so, Donner, I just hope so. That's why we have to keep alert every minute."

Jim checked the safe handle, twirled the knob on the combination and then followed the sergeant out the door.

They found a soldier guard slumped between the cars. The trooper had been stabbed in the chest, the blade going into a lung, Jim was sure. He was still alive but not by much.

"How in hell . . ." the sergeant began. Then he helped Jim carry the trooper into the passenger car and laid him on the first seat, his legs dangling in the aisle.

"Doctor Carter!" Jim bellowed, and the small man was there almost at once. He

140

looked at the stab wound and the bleeding and shook his head.

"This is bad, I'll need some help."

Mandy moved beside him and knelt near the seat. "I can help, doctor. I'm good patching up ducks with broken legs and good at taking care of new foals."

The doctor nodded and checked the soldiers eyes, then his pulse and his breathing.

Jim was surprised to see Mandy up and moving. He patted her shoulder and decided it was past time he made a thorough search of the whole train. He had to find Billings. The man was still on board, Jim was sure now. Billings had knifed the trooper after Jim had gone by him into the baggage car not three minutes before.

As long as Billings was on board, everyone was in danger. Jim stared at the baggage car door, checked on top of the train, but found only the trooper stationed there. Inside the first coach he looked under every seat, behind every possible hiding spot. He did not find Billings. Jim sat down in a train seat for a moment. Where could Billings be hiding? In this car were the passengers and the guards. Maybe the next car? No, Billings had fled from the soldiers, he wouldn't go back in there, they would spot him at once.

Jim moved down to where the wounded trooper lay. He was conscious, holding on. Mandy wiped his forehead, then put a damp towel on it. She was talking to the soldier softly, telling him they were taking care of him.

Dr. Carter motioned Jim up the aisle and spoke quietly, urgently.

"We have to get him off the train and to a hospital where he can be cared for properly, I'm not sure how bad the wound is, but it could kill him. If it penetrated the lung very far, it is extremely dangerous."

"Doctor, there's no hospital near us, and I don't know where the next one is down the line, but it's a long, long ways."

"He's probably bleeding internally. There's nothing I can do for him this way, just make him as comfortable as possible. I have some pain killer if he gets hurting too much." He lifted his hands. "That's about all I can do without operating, and on this jiggling, bouncing train . . ."

"Anything else you need?"

"Some blankets. We can cushion him a little more and keep him warm, I know it's a warm day, still he's chilled, a body re-action."

"I'll try to borrow some blankets." Jim

shook the doctor's hand. "I'm grateful for what you're doing. I just wish there was more we could do for the boy."

Jim went on through the coach looking at the passengers, hoping some might have extra blankets. He found only two which he took back to the doctor.

In the next car he reminded the sergeant about the missing prisoner, assured the men the gambler was still on board, and told them to keep an eye out for him.

"Sergeant, you better go back and stay with your trooper. He's in bad shape."

The sergeant's face clouded, and he pushed his tan campaign hat back on his head. "I better not lose that boy. He's one of my good ones."

"The doctor is trying, believe me. Sarge, if you were going to hide on a train, where would it be?"

"There ain't one hell of a lot of spots, are there? And I'd guess you checked them all. Might help to ask the conductor up there. He almost passed out when the lead was flying I hear, but he should know his own train."

Jim hadn't seen the conductor for a while. The man was sleeping in the last seat at the front of the car. He had two blankets draped over him. Jim slid one blanket off, and tossed it to Sgt. Southdown. "Take this to your man," Jim said. Then he woke up the trainman.

"Yeah, uh, yeah, what time is it? Oh?" The sleepy conductor said coming out of it. Then he saw Jim and stood quickly. "Just getting forty winks between stations. Any more trouble?"

"Yes. We've got a killer on board. Where could he be hiding?"

The conductor, whose name was Franklin, lifted his brows.

"A killer?"

"Probably. One of the troopers was knifed. What about that little room at the end of this car? The other car doesn't have one like it."

"Oh, that's train gear, storage, and it's been locked."

"Let's look at it," Jim said.

They did. The lock was intact, and there was no one inside, and nowhere Billings could hide. The conductor locked the door.

"I'll watch for him, Jim. That's the best I can do."

"And he can't get in the boxcar up front?"

"It's locked and sealed, and ahead of that is the tender and the engine. Your roof guard would see him if he tried to get over that way."

Jim went back to the passenger car and checked on the soldier. He was alive but coughing and the doctor was worried. Once he coughed up blood.

A half hour later Jim sat beside Mandy who held the trooper's hand and talked to him, even though he couldn't hear her. He had lapsed into unconsciousness again.

The train had been climbing steadily and was now deep into the mountains. They came to a narrow valley that had waving grass growing in a meadow on both sides of the tracks. Suddenly horsemen came out of the timber on both sides and men were shooting at the train.

"Everyone down!" Jim bellowed. "Men, get your rifles out!"

Jim saw horsemen on both sides of the train riding hard and firing as they came. Windows splintered again. Bullets whined into the car. Someone inside screamed.

Jim grabbed a repeating rifle and began firing back. The other troopers and the civilian guards were shooting as well. The firepower on the train was enough to hold them off, Jim figured. At least twenty repeating rifles. Jim led one rider and fired, knocking the man off the horse. The train was gaining on the riders. Gradually the train pulled ahead of the attackers and Jim thought they were through the worst of it. But suddenly the train slowed and the horsemen surged forward, firing as they came.

More windows shattered and Mandy bent low, lying across the soldier, protecting him.

The train slowed more and more until at last it came to a stop. Jim kept firing out a broken window, and trying to figure out what had happened.

Jim wanted to jump off the train and run to the engine to see what the trouble was. But with the firing outside he knew he would never make it. He kept the rifle busy and realized the attackers had mostly pistols, with only two or three rifles.

The rifle fire continued from the stopped train, and now the trooper and the men on the train had the advantage. The train wasn't moving, the marksmen could pick their shots easier and with more accuracy. The civilian and military rifles poured out fire and within five minutes the attack from the raiders was beaten off. The last of the attackers rode hard for the trees with a shower of lead to urge them on.

Jim swung off the train and ran forward to the engine. What the hell had happened up there?

CHAPTER 10

Jim stepped into the cab of the locomotive, his sixgun in hand and for a moment he had trouble believing what he saw. Blood was everywhere. On the cab floor sat Josh, his cocked pistol aimed at Jim's head. As soon as he could see the person coming up the steps, Josh lowered his gun, and Jim saw Amos Handshoe's head lay cradled in Josh's blood drenched lap.

"The bastard shot him!" Josh screamed. "They rode up beside the cab, waved at him, then this one guy on a pinto horse shot Amos right in the throat. Amos fell down and his foot came off the pedal and we started slowing down. The bastards! I hope you killed all of them!"

Josh tenderly put Amos's head on the steel floor of the cab, jumped to the right-of-way and ran fifty yards into the valley and stood there. Jim knew that Josh was crying.

Jim waved to the conductor to come up.

They met halfway along the train and Jim told him what happened.

"My God, he had four kids," Franklin said. "I'll get a blanket and we'll put him in the storage area in that first passenger car. No way we can leave him out here. Got to take his body back to Denver."

It took them a half hour to get the body moved and the blood cleaned off the floor so a man could stand on the metal plates without slipping.

Josh had come back to the cab. He looked at Jim for a long time then he nodded.

"Reckon I'm the only one aboard who can run this bitch. You send me two men, both with repeating rifles. I want one to stand guard all the time and the other one to stoke the boiler. You do that and I'll see if we can get this devil train on into Denver."

Five minutes later Jim had positioned two of his civilian guards in the train cab, told them to take turns stoking the fire and standing guard duty.

"Anything Josh here tells you to do, you do it and do it damn fast," Jim said. "He's the ramrod up here and what he says is law. If you see anybody with a gun riding outside the cab, shoot the bastard first and we'll argue about who got killed later."

By this time everyone on the train knew

the engineer had been shot and killed. One of the civilian guards Jim had brought from the mine had taken a ricocheting bullet in the arm. The slug went in sideways and plowed on through. His upper arm was torn up badly, but Dr. Carter was on the job, sewing it back together, splashing it with wood alcohol. He had a soldier sloshing the alcohol on it every few seconds. He said it was something called "antiseptic," which Jim didn't quite understand. He decided it should do the job as well as whiskey. When the alcohol first hit the open wound, the soldier had screamed and passed out. Dr. Carter nodded and went to work.

Jim swung into the passenger car and almost at once Mandy flew down the aisle and began beating on his chest with her fists.

"Damn, damn, damn!" she shouted, then she moaned, and began crying. She clung to him, her face pressed into his shirt as she sobbed.

"The soldier died, didn't he Mandy?"

She nodded. "He was hurt so badly, he did well to hold on as long as he did. There was just nothing the doctor could do for him."

She went right on sobbing. Jim picked her up and put her in a rear seat, tucked the dress around her feet and pointed her face to the window.

"You just sit there for a while and watch the scenery and remember that you did as much as you could for him. That you made his going as easy as possible. Not all of those ducks with broken wings you doctored lived, did they, Mandy?"

She sighed and shook her head, then she tried to stop the tears from coming.

"But he was so young to die. He wasn't much older than I am, and now he's gone. He's dead."

"Mandy, enough of that. Just try to think how pretty the country is, and that's an order." He stood and watched her for a moment, then walked on up the car.

A woman in her forties traveling with a man about the same age grabbed his sleeve as he came next to her. She wore a hat, and a dress, both black, and an expression that was similar. Her gray eyes shot sparks at him from over a hooked nose.

"Young man, you seem to be in charge here. We hear all the trouble on this train is because you've got a fortune in gold back in the baggage car. You have no right to risk our lives just so you can get your gold to Denver. We know it's going to the mint there. The railroad should have used a special train for that. When I get to Denver

I'm going to demand that the Union Pacific be hauled into court and made to pay plenty for all of the inconvenience, the danger, and the pain this trip has already cost father and me."

"I don't work for the railroad, ma'am," Jim said and went on past her. He was certain the next big shipment of gold that went by rail would have its own little train with no passengers, only guards.

Jim kept looking for Billings. The gambler and killer had to be on board somewhere. Jim studied the face of every man in the car. He had put all of his civilian guards next to the windows and in otherwise vacant seats. That put the women and men passengers nearest the aisle where they could get out of the way as quickly as possible. Jim studied each man as he went up the car. Not one of them was even the right size for Billings. So he couldn't be disguised and sitting right there in the passenger car. He took a quick look at the small bathroom at the far end of the car but no one was there and no one could hide in the small area.

Jim continued through and climbed the steel rung to the roof. An Army trooper lay there in his blue shirt and pants, wiping smoke out of his eyes. The wind brought the smoke and ashes from the engine straight back along the train, since there wasn't enough wind to blow it to one side. Then the train turned and the wind blew the smoke away and they both could see again. Jim stood and looked ahead at the tracks for as far as the next curve let him see. They they were around that curve and he saw smoke but not from the engine.

"Indians?" the trooper asked, bringing up his rifle.

"Forest fire?" Jim wondered out loud.

They watched as the train wound around two more gentle curves as it kept climbing. The tracks straightened out then ahead and a half mile up the rails Jim saw the fire. Someone had piled logs directly on the tracks and set them on fire. He wondered how many five-gallon cans of kerosene they had poured on the logs to get them burning. It had taken two or three hours to get the fire going good, Jim was sure of that. Jim ran ahead on top of the passenger car, then over the next one and across the freight car to the tender. He was in the cab of the locomotive a few seconds later.

"I seen it, I seen it," Josh said as Jim jumped into the cab. Jim had alerted the men in the train by sending a roof sentry down to explain what was going on. He saw rifles stick out of the passenger car windows.

"Somebody wants to stop us again," Jim said.

Josh stared at the log pile. "I'm trying to decide if we can blast our way through it, or if they have some rails torn up, or if they just want us to slow down considerable."

"Can we push on through?"

"If it's nothing but those burning logs. And if they don't have one lengthways between the tracks like that first one, then we probably could."

Jim watched as they moved closer. Josh had reduced power and the engine crawled up the hill toward the blockade.

"We'll edge up to it and take a better look. If nobody starts shooting we can nudge the pile and see what happens."

They were within a hundreds yards of the burning logs now and the stack looked bigger. Logs were piled six feet high on the tracks, with some angled up twenty feet into the air. The roaring fire bed on the bottom looked like it had been burning for days. Jim was sure there wouldn't be any ties along there.

The train crept closer. Josh stopped the engine when it was twenty feet from the pile. They could feel the heat even at that distance.

"It's too much," Josh said. "We can't risk

hitting it fast, and if we try to nudge it off slowly, we're bound to burn up in the try."

The train was dead on the tracks now, the brakes holding it in place.

They all felt the lurch of the train at the same time. Josh knew what it meant.

"Damn, somebody disconnected part of the cars in back. Take a look!"

Jim jumped to the ground and ran. In back of the freight car he saw the first passenger coach sliding away from him. He ran hard, caught the rear bar and swung up on the steps.

The conductor was at the door, unlocking it, trying to hold down the anger and fear.

"Runaway!" was all Franklin could say. He looked as if he were ready to throw up.

Jim shook him, then slapped his face.

"Come on, Franklin. You're the trainman. What should we do?"

"We have thirty miles behind us all downhill," Franklin said. "We roll and roll until we get going so fast that we derail, go over the side into some canyon on a curve and smash all of us right into hell!"

"How do we stop it?" Jim yelled. "How? How can we stop this thing?"

"Hand brakes," the conductor said.

"Where?"

The conductor pointed to the eighteen

inch diameter wheel at the top of the passenger car. Jim rushed up the rungs of the ladder and began turning the wheel to the right. He moved it a turn and a half then it stopped.

"Harder," Franklin said. "It turns damn hard."

Jim tried, then told Franklin to go into the train and put one man on each of the hand brakes. They had to try to slow down the cars. Jim went back to the brake, pulling harder, inched the wheel around, and he felt the car slow a little. At least they weren't speeding up as much. They came to a curve and the cars swung around it faster than normal, but they stayed on the tracks.

Franklin was back.

"We're doing all we can. Our only hope is to cut loose the last three cars, get the soldiers in this passenger car. Then we cut loose the other passenger, the baggage car and the caboose. That will cut our weight and we might be able to stop this one car. Maybe!"

Jim thought about it. They could get all the people out and let the gold car go. No! He was going to deliver that gold to Denver as ordered.

"Get the brakeman out and let the caboose go," Jim said. "That will help us a little. Get another man up here on this brake. No, put two soldiers on each brake. Use the rifles as levers if they have to. Slow down this damn train!"

Jim stepped to the top of the car and ran toward the caboose. He saw the frightened face of the brakeman as he climbed down.

"Runaway!" the brakeman said.

"Any idea how we can stop this lobo?" Jim asked.

"Hell no. I was just looking for a soft spot to jump off."

"We're uncoupling the caboose. Come on, you know how to do it and we're doing it now."

"Not without authorization from the conductor. It's his responsibility."

"What's your name?"

"Jim Gatling."

"Well, Franklin just told me to tell you to do it." Jim drew his .45. "And here's the rest of the authorization. If you don't do it right now, I'm shooting you through the kneecap. What is it, disconnect or limp for the rest of your life?"

They went over the top of the caboose and down between the cars. Jim stayed on the roof of the baggage car as the brakeman disconnected the two cars. The caboose rolled a dozen feet away and slowed. They caught it and almost bumped into it, then the caboose rolled faster and moved away from them down the tracks.

A curve was coming up. The caboose went around it easily, but the passenger cars weaved and the rails screeched as the wheels pressed with unusual pressure on them.

The grade increased, and the cars rolled faster. Ahead they saw another curve, not as bad as the last one. Jim tensed sitting on top of the baggage car as he watched the caboose a quarter of a mile down the tracks. It hit the curve, and the caboose tilted outward.

Jim watched in fascination as the wheels lifted off the tracks on the inside, then simply raised higher and higher until the whole caboose rolled off the tracks, the wheels catching on a tie, then catapaulted forward, twisting and rolling all the time until it hit in the gully below the tracks, then rolled and rolled, breaking up as it went side over side down the long slope.

"I hope it didn't tear up the tracks when it went off," Gatling said. "Lots of times a derailing like that will. We'll know in about sixty seconds."

They both held on as the baggage car rocketed toward the same curve where the caboose had vaulted off the tracks.

"This is it!" Jim yelled and hung on.

They rolled over the spot and felt no difference at all. They were going fast enough so there was more than the regular sway.

"Back to work on the brakes," Jim said. They struggled, turning the hand brake as hard as they could. Up the line of small cars they saw pairs of men on each end of the other cars doing the same thing. Almost imperceptibly the cars began to slow. The next curve was easier, with almost no sway. The clicking of the rail joints came slightly slower now. Jim looked down the tracks and started to laugh.

They were on a flat place, or perhaps a slight incline. Any little rise would be enough to stop them. That coupled with the effect of the hand brake's pressure should stop the runaway dead still.

The brakeman sensed it too and he grinned.

"Yeah, now my biggest problem is that we may all not die after all," Gatling said. "But that brings on another problem. All my food is still in that caboose up the tracks."

"I'll buy you lunch," Jim said, grinning and pulling harder on the brake wheel. He was pushing the spokes with his boots now, as the string of three cars rolled slower and slower.

"Almost got her," Gatling said.

"No we haven't!" Jim said. "Look out there."

When Gatling turned so he could see the tracks again he frowned.

"We're slanting downhill, I thought that flat place was long enough."

"Afraid not. We're picking up speed again."

Jim knew he should have had all the civilians get off the train when it had almost stopped. But it was too late for that now.

Then he heard a train whistle. It came from far up the tracks toward Denver.

"That's Josh on the whistle cord," Gatling said. "He's coming after us. But he can't back up that rig too fast or he'll lose it and then we'll have two runaways. At least he has the engine's brakes to use."

"How can he help us?" Jim asked.

"As soon as he catches up to that first passenger car he bangs the coupler on the freight car into the passenger car and they hook up, he grabs us and stops us."

"Yeah, if he can catch us," Jim said. "Push on that damn wheel!"

The cars crept ahead faster, then faster yet as the slant of the tracks increased. They heard the whistle again, closer this time.

"God damn, look down there," Gatling said.

The pitch of the downgrade increased, and below they could see a sharper curve than any they had come to before.

"We'll be lucky if we can stay on the tracks around that one," the brakeman said.

"We're gonna try," Jim shouted back. "If we do, we all live a little longer."

Now both men were using their feet on the spokes of the big flat wheel, yet the cars seemed to be gaining in speed. They heard the whistle of the engine.

"I remember this stretch," Gatling said. "There's a curve down there that they slow down to take *coming up!* We couldn't ever swing that one at this speed."

"Look," Jim yelled.

The end of the box car nosed around the curve up the tracks from them and the engine was right behind it, spouting a steady stream of black angry smoke from the stacks. The train seemed to spurt toward them.

"Damn that Josh is gonna dump the engine, then we'll all be in one hell of a spot," Gatling said, his voice brimming with enthusiasm. "Look at that son of a bitch push that engine!"

The wheels on the passenger cars

screeched as they pressed against the sides of the rails dangerously hard, then they were around the first smaller curve and Jim swore loudly.

"There's your sharp curve. We'll never hold on that one."

A quarter of a mile ahead the tracks vanished to the left, making a sudden turn on a shelf of rock that had been blasted away from the side of the cliff.

"That's the curve I was telling you about," Gatling said.

"Come on, Josh!" Jim yelled.

The engine and its still coupled freight car came forward again, too fast. Soon the box car would slam into the first passenger car. Jim hoped it didn't hit it so hard it derailed them all and bounced them into the gully.

Jim watched the cars ahead, then saw someone climb up on the back of the freight car, he evidently was signaling to Josh.

The brakeman yelled. "Hold on, Jim, we're gonna get hit!"

Jim held tightly just as the box car coupler hit the first passenger car coupler and all the other cars down the line felt the jolting union.

But it didn't hook up.

"He's going to try it again," Gatling said.

The bad curve was only two hundred yards away.

The box car hit the passenger car coupler again, and this time there was only a short jolt and the brakeman cheered.

"God damn, he's done it, we're hooked up!"

Almost at once Josh must have cut power on the engine and applied the engine's powerful brakes. They could hear the screeching of the raw steel wheels on the polished rails and the whole train shuddered as weights and forces shifted. But it slowed.

Jim reached over and shook hands with the brakemen. He didn't know what else to do.

They watched the curve come up now, saw how sharp it was, how little room the engineers had to work with. They watched fascinated by the sharp angle and the speed and felt the train moving slower and slower. The baggage car rounded the first part of the curve then the car shuddered to a stop. With hardly a pause they heard the engine's power feed to the big wheels and the pistons spun the wheels on the steel for a moment, then they took hold and the train began to move forward again.

Jim looked at the brakeman and nodded,

then both men ran along the top of the car to where they could get inside.

CHAPTER 11

Jim Steel dropped down to the plate between the two rail cars and turned into the
passenger coach. Mandy spotted him as
soon as he came through the door and ran
to him, a strange look on her pretty face.
She stopped two paces away and stared at
Jim. He couldn't read her face. Was it anger,
frustration, or suspicion.

"Sometimes I wonder about you, Jim
Steel," she said, her tone even but not quite
accusing. "I wonder if you're the one behind
all this trouble getting the gold through. You
can give the company a run, cause problems, make it look good, then suddenly van-
ish with the baggage car and all the gold
and we never see you again. You could probably do it."

Then she sighed, the dimples popped in
as she smiled. "But I really don't believe
that." She rushed forward and hugged him
tightly. Jim pecked a kiss on her cheek.

"Now, that sounds like the Mandy Martindale that I know, feisty, illogical and cute as a spotted fawn on a dewy morning. Glad to see you back to normal. Got any sandwiches left."

"You can think of food at a time like this."

"True, I can."

"I've got a couple, but only if you tell me how you stopped our runaway train."

"I didn't stop it. And twelve of us were working on the hand brakes at the end of each car. Then Josh came roaring back with the engine and caught us, coupled with the first car and stopped us. Another quarter mile and we'd all be lying down in some canyon busted up, smashed to pieces and dead or worse."

"So Josh really saved the runaway?"

"Yes."

"He's the fireman who took over when the engineer . . ."

"Right."

"Then he gets a bonus. I want you to pay him a thousand dollars when we get to Denver. Daddy will pay it back to you."

Jim grinned. "I'd be glad to, he deserves it. Now where's that sandwich?" They ate the last two sandwiches in silence. Then Mandy looked up.

"I really didn't mean to accuse you of trying to steal the gold. I just had to say something. I was so frightened. And I get mad easy, did you know that."

"I'm finding out." He stood. "Thanks for the eats, I've got to get up front. We'll be coming to that bonfire place again soon and it's still trouble."

Jim was ready for the bonfire barricade this time. He had talked it over with Sgt. Southdown and the veteran agreed. Jim stepped off the train as the string of cars slowed. He jumped to the shoulder and six troopers got off behind Jim. The men fanned out at five yard intervals across the cleared right of way next to the tracks and kept pace with the train as it neared the bonfire still burning on the tracks. A similar group swept along the other side of the train under command of Sgt. Southdown. When the train stopped, two civilian riflemen moved to each train coupling and stood guard, weapons ready.

Jim ran toward the fire. It had mostly subsided, but still presented a problem. It could have weakened the rails, maybe even softened the steel, and the wooden ties that held the rails in place might have burned away. Even with the fire almost out, the train might spread the rails too much so the engine couldn't get over them. Jim brought his squad beyond the fire and secured the area in front of the small blaze. They saw no horses, no men, no signs that anyone had been there.

Jim motioned them down into prone positions, behind trees, or rocks, and all pointing outward to form a secure perimeter.

He made sure there was no long log lying between the rails, then went to the other side of the fire and found Josh.

"How does it look?" Jim asked.

"Tough. All we can do is try to get across it. We should have a crew here to put in new rails and make sure. It's the rails I'm worried about now. We can push the little pile of burning sticks and logs out of the way. But if those rails got hot enough to soften, we could drop into the roadbed."

"So let's try it," Jim said.

"Right now before it gets dark," Josh put in. "We should have about half an hour of daylight left."

The sun was down, and dusk was coming. Josh jumped back in the cab and drove the train ahead at a crawl. The brakeman walked beside the heavy wheels yelling a continual report to Josh.

"Rails are fine, keep her coming. No problem yet. The engine is the heaviest part, we get her over and we'll be riding home free and clear."

The cow catcher hit the first burning log and pushed it to one side, then another. The wheels came to the center of the fire area, and Gatling yelled.

"Easy! This is the touchy part. Some of the ties are burned in half, some are gone. Tracks are sinking, maybe four to six inches. Okay, yes, keep it coming. No spread at least. Looking fine so far, tracks are holding true. Move it, keep it going, yes, looks fine."

Another log rolled from where the fire had been, down the right of way into the cleared area to the sides of the track. It smoldered but would be no danger.

The men at the couplings kept up their guard, moving along with the train. It took ten minutes, but finally the last car had edged past the burn spot on the tracks.

Josh stopped the train just beyond and Gatling took his small wooden box and climbed a telegraph pole that had been marching along beside the tracks. He cut into the telegraph wire and tapped out a message to everyone on the line warning them about the fire on the tracks and asking for a repair crew. If a train hit the spot at speed it could derail.

Ten minutes after darkness fell, the train was back up to speed, pounding down the tracks. Jim sat beside Mandy shaking his head.

"Somebody is spending one hell of a lot of money to try to stop us," Jim said. "I'd like to see a total on his expense sheet."

"For half a million in gold it might be worth it," she said.

Jim shook his head. "It can't be worth it if even one man gets killed. Already we've had two killed, and the other side must have lost five or six. It can't be worth that much."

With the dark they had lighted gas jets in the car, and now a flickering pale illumination came through. Most of the passengers had settled down to try to sleep. Jim kept the guards on two shifts, half sleeping, half ready and awake.

It was nearly an hour later and they were nearing the Nevada border when one of the lookouts on the roof of the passenger car dropped down and opened the back door. Jim was on his feet at once walking to meet the soldier.

"Trouble?" Jim asked.

"I don't know, sir. Come and look."

On the roof Jim stared ahead when the trooper pointed and saw a dull red glow.

"Forest fire," Jim said. "That looks like a real one. You stay here and keep alert." Jim ran down the roof of the swaying car, jumped to the next passenger car and went along his route to the engine cab. Inside Josh had not yet seen the red glow.

"If it's a forest fire, we want to know in plenty of time," Josh said. "I don't aim to get burned to a cinder inside this iron coffin."

They watched as the train climbed the grade. When the engine topped a small rise and rolled along another mile, they could see the fire. It wasn't huge like some Jim had seen when twenty miles were burning. But this one was directly ahead and now obviously burning on both sides of the tracks.

" 'Pears like it does cross the rails," Josh said. "If it does, we got to stop and wait for it to burn itself out."

They moved another mile, and Josh slowed the train. They were coming to a narrow valley, with peaks on both sides.

"You notice much wind out there?" Josh asked.

"It's blowing with us, a caboose wind," Jim said.

"Good," Josh said. The two soldiers stood by, one feeding wood into the fire when it needed it. The train was within a mile of the fire, now, and the men could see sudden flames roar up a pine tree as it gushed with fire, then the brightness faded and the brush continued to burn below. Even with the wind blowing away from them, they could smell the smoke.

"I'm going to stop about half a mile ahead," Josh said. "You better get your guards put out. We don't want anybody unlocking any more cars."

Jim went over the tender and back to the first passenger car and inside. He told Sgt. Southdown about the stop and had him put his troopers on guard duty around the couplings and the engine. They used six civilian guards as well as the soldiers.

Jim felt the train jolt to a stop and a moment later a woman screamed at the other end of the second passenger car. Jim turned and raced down past the stove to where a man lay in the aisle. His throat had been cut and he was dead. There was little bleeding, and Jim guessed the man had been dead for some time. The sudden jolting stop of the train had tipped him out of his seat.

The man sitting behind the dead man paled as he spoke.

"I thought he was sleeping. He wasn't a big talker. I went to the rest room and when I came back he was like that, sitting there with his chin down. I guess he didn't move since then."

"Anybody see the person sitting beside him?" Jim asked. A woman and two men close by shrugged. They had been sleeping or eating most of the time, and looking out the window before it got dark. Jim examined the body. It was a neat, professional job, first the slash across the throat so the man couldn't talk or cry out, then a thrust into the heart to kill him. But why would the gambler kill this man, a mere passenger? That was supposing that the gambler were still on board, and that he did the killing. The victim must have recognized the gambler, or saw him do something the gambler didn't want him talking about. Whatever it was it cost the passenger his life.

Jim picked up the body and carried it forward to the second passenger coach and had the conductor put it in with the other bodies, in the storage room. It was looking like a battlefield morgue.

Jim turned back toward the baggage car. He was going to make one good inspection in there again. There was a chance the gambler could be there, but not a very large one. He had to do something. This sitting around was starting to worry him. The clerk and two of his civilians were on guard and the door was sturdy and locked. That should cover that problem.

Outside the stopped train guards stood near the coupling on each car, their weapons cocked and ready. They could smell the fire now, see places where fingers of the greedy flames had burned toward the tracks, but ran out of fuel and left only a black, snake track of sooty destruction.

Jim was talking to two of his civilian guards near the last car when he heard an explosion. It shattered the stillness of the night and all Jim could think of was the baggage car. He wondered if it could be a signal for someone out there in the woods to charge the car. Jim raced down the right of way to the baggage car and jumped up the steps. The door hung by one hinge where it had been blown inward. One of the guards on the outside had been nicked by flying glass. Jim drew his sixgun and moved cautiously into the car. Smoke hung thick and choking in the stale air. Jim tried to see through it, then groped his way toward the safe. He stumbled and fell. When he looked back at what he stumbled over he saw the postal clerk. Jim crawled to him and rolled him over. Then he swore.

A knife stuck from Donner's chest. Jim touched his neck and Donner's eyes fluttered open. At least he was still alive.

"Who, Donner? Who did it?" Jim asked.

Donner licked his lips, tried to swallow. "Wo . . . Wom . . ."

His eyes closed again, then slowly opened. Donner shuddered, his face twisted in an agonizing grimace, then he relaxed and licked his lips again.

"Wo . . . Wom . . ."

"Yes, I got that part, is it a name? What does that mean, Donner?"

Donner stared at him for a moment, then his eyes faded to gray and the pupils almost vanished, as his head slowly rolled to one side and his eyelids closed, then fell open as Donner stared at death and could not look away.

Jim watched Donner for another few seconds. When he was sure Donner was dead, Jim crawled to the safe and looked at it. It was secure. The blast had blown out one of the gas lights, but the second still burned as the air began to clear of the smoke and the sulphur smell of the dynamite. He heard one guard moaning near the door. Then someone came at Jim from the gloom at the far end of the wall. Jim pulled up his sixgun, then saw it was one of the guards from the mine.

Jim turned toward the moan and found the other guard on the floor near the side of the car. He had worked up to a sitting posi-

174

tion but now groaned and held his head. Jim knelt down beside him and the man nodded, his eyes seeming to focus now.

"Jim . . . I don't know what it was. Something hit me alongside the head and knocked me over here. I'd been by the door. I must have passed out. I really don't know what happened."

The other civilian stood beside Jim.

"He was near the door on guard duty. The door must have hit him when it blew. I saw some kind of a shape come rushing in after the blast. Then I heard Donner yell. Is Donner hurt?"

"He's dead, knifed."

"Oh, my God!"

"Where were you when the door blew?" Jim asked the second guard.

"I was sleeping, sawing off logs back there by the baggage on some empty mail sacks. Until the door blew. When my ears stopped ringing I got up."

Jim had them help him. They had to get a barricade up over the door to protect it. There was no chance that the door could be fixed or put back in place. He lit the other gas lamp in the car that had been blown out, then they moved a trunk in front of the gaping open doorway. They put another trunk on top of it and then brought up a third one. The injured guard said he was all right, he'd be sore but nothing was broken, he wasn't even bleeding.

"Stay on the alert. I want both of you awake now for the next two hours, then you'll be relieved."

Jim crawled over the trunks to the outside, and the men shoved the third small trunk into the opening, sealing off the car.

"Nobody gets in there, you hear?" Jim called. "If anybody except me tries to get in, put a shot into that bottom trunk."

The guards said they would and Jim left the car, jumping down to the roadbed. Outside the car he walked the length of the short train checking the guards on the couplers. No one had seen a thing. No forces had stormed out of the blackened trees. Everything was quiet. Jim wondered if the unseen enemy had started the forest fire to stop them, or if it had been an accident of nature, a lightning strike, perhaps.

At the cab Josh was impatient.

"I don't like sitting out here waiting for somebody to take a shot at us, Jim," the substitute engineer said. He looked ahead at the fire. The main part of the blaze had swung up the ridge to the left. The tracks ran along the bottom of the valley which had been burned out.

"Looks like we can give it a try. I think most of the fire has shifted away from the tracks. Now, if it didn't burn up half the ties, we should be able to work our way through. Tell the people to hang on, we're going to try it."

Jim ran back to the first passenger car. "As soon as we get moving, jump on board," he told the guards on the way. Then he was inside, told the people they were moving out again. Jim concentrated on the men and their faces. Only one had a thin face, and only that one was large enough to be the gambler Forrest Billings. The trouble was the man was in his sixties, with a whitish, scraggly beard that couldn't be a fake.

Jim sat down beside Mandy.

"The blast, did it hurt anything?" she asked.

"The door to the baggage car is gone, but we'll make out. Do you know anybody on board with a name starting with a W, something like Wo or Wom . . . Womack, maybe. Anything like that?"

"I only know one person's name, Mrs. Beloit. That probably won't help much. Why?"

"Just wondering," he said. Jim sat there staring out the window at the blackness. Wo . . . Wom . . . What did it mean? What was the dying postal clerk trying to tell him?

CHAPTER 12

Brad Smith pushed the crushed Stetson back on his head and wiped his forehead as he waited in the moonlight. He was nervous, but that was good. He always liked to be a little worked up and on edge before a big fight. And this would be a fight, he was sure of that. He was a big man with red hair, a slack jaw and hard, green eyes. He lay now behind the supports of the water tower, on the Union Pacific line at the Ft. Ruby siding. The stop here was ten miles distant from the fort, but that was because the fort was put in first for the best military position. The railroad men came much later and picked the best right of way.

Smith spat a shot of tobacco juice into the night. The army detail from Ft. Ruby was supposed to be there at eight o'clock. The Army was late as usual. In his three years in the other army it had always been late too. Now he hadn't worn a uniform for almost ten years. Smith spat brown juice again and looked over his neat little ambush. His ten men were spread out on the near side of the flag stop, with all of them positioned so no one would shoot at anyone on his side. Smith had a fine crossfire plan set up and he was anxious to see it go into operation. If it worked the way it was supposed to, all ten of the army trash would be dead in the first volley.

Smith wasn't sure what this mission was all about. The money was right, two hundred and fifty dollars for him and twenty-five dollars for each of the nine men he hired for the three day's work. It was an offer he could not let move on down the trail.

His specific instructions were to capture or kill the army patrol of ten men without messing up their uniforms. That shouldn't be much of a problem.

A few minutes later he heard hoofbeats on the trail, and the jangle of saddles and equipment. Smith grinned. This detail had not been told to rig for silent movement. He gave a low night hawk call and heard a poor meadowlark response. Everything was ready.

The army sergeant leading the nine other cavalrymen had been ordered into the job tonight when the man who volunteered to lead the detail came down sick. Sgt. Banning wasn't happy about it, even if it did mean a break in routine and two days leave in Denver. He'd just as soon ride his army saddle on his army mount. The sergeant shrugged. That was the army for you, surprises, surprises.

Sgt. Banning led his men around the bend in the trail and saw the siding ahead in the moonlight. At least their horses would be picked up and ridden back to the fort by the ten men they were relieving. He turned in his McClelland army issue saddle and watched the last three men in the detail come into the clearing near the tracks. They would tie their mounts to the hitching rail and be ready for the train. It was supposed to be there at 8:15, but it was late, as usual.

Sgt. Banning turned once more to check the men when he heard a night hawk's call. It was the strangest sounding night hawk he had ever heard. The flash and report came almost at the same time before the .45 caliber rifle bullet entered Sgt. Banning's chest, smashed through a rib and plowed sideways through his heart, turning this short ride to the Ft. Ruby siding into his ticket to eternity.

As his dead body slammed backward off the horse, his right spur caught in the stirrup and the army mount bolted, dragging Sgt. Banning's body forty yards toward the water tower.

A second later after the first rifle shot, nine more shots blasted into the night. Five troopers went down and were dead or dying, two others were wounded. One man fell from his horse on purpose as soon as he heard the first shot. Billy Joe Zack lay still near his horse, not moving a finger. He hoped the ambushers had taken their eyes off him. Five seconds later he squirmed into a ditch and crawled as fast as he could staying low to the mother earth as all hell broke loose around him.

A horse charged past him, jumped the ditch and fled into the trees. A trooper surged up and fired once with his carbine, then threw himself down.

To Zack's left a man screamed in pain and frustration as he lay dying. A horse near Zack shrieked in mortal pain as it tried to raise its useless hind quarters, then slowly lost control of its front legs and died in a flurry of weaker and weaker front leg kicks.

The second trooper behind Sgt. Banning caught a round in the shoulder, spinning him off his horse. He had time only to grab for his carbine as he tumbled to the ground. For a moment he was unconscious, then he came to swearing. He pulled up his carbine with one hand and began firing at the flashes in the woods across the no man's land of the tracks.

A round grazed his head and the man screamed in protest. He lifted his carbine, stood up and fired, charging the rifles in the woods. Three bullets hit him almost at once, robbing him of life and dropping him to the ground sprawled in a silent contortion.

The other two soldiers who survived the first volley remained near the tracks and now were pinned down in a small depression. They waited for the enemy's charge. One man screamed at the ambushers, calling them murderers, challenging them, but there was no answer. The man crouched, dove, and rolled toward a ditch. Two slugs caught him as he moved in the moonlight. He died as he rolled, his eyes looking at the woods, still unable to find his enemy, his tormentors.

The other man, Corporal Hawkins, shook his head in fury at the wild try his friend had taken. He lay still, knowing the enemy could not hit him from where they were. He had earned his stripes by using his head, which he continued to do. For just a second he saw a head appear beyond the tracks around a tree trunk. Almost at once it vanished. Cpl. Hawkins aimed his army Springfield carbine at the spot and when the same man lifted up again, Hawkins fired and smiled with satisfaction as he saw the big. 45 round blow the man's face apart and hurl him backward into hell.

Brad Smith had worked his way through the fringe of woods well beyond where he knew the last army trooper lay. Now he had a wider angle at the depression and could see in the side of it. Smith waited, he had just as much patience as the army man had. When at last Cpl. Hawkins moved to ease his legs, Smith could see enough of the man for a shot. Smith fired twice as quickly as he could. One of the slugs ripped through the man's side and smashed his spine killing him instantly.

"That should do it, boys," Smith called. "I'll check." He ran fast and low to the deadly site, examined the bodies and swore when he could find only nine dead men. Evidently one got away. There wasn't much the man could do. He didn't ride back to the fort, because Smith could see all ten horses around the area. The lone trooper might try to warn the train. Smith would watch for him.

"Come on, you no-good bastards! Get up here and get busy!" Smith bellowed. "Pick out a man nearest your size and get him into the brush and change clothes. You farts have to at least look like soldiers in the dark. Get a move on. I don't know how much more time we got. And be sure to move the bodies far enough back into the woods so nobody can see them from the train. Get your blue suits on and them stovepipe boots and be sure you find all the army carbines. We'll have to use them. Move it, you guys!"

Smith sent one man to run down the horses and tie them military style at the hitching rail.

Billy Joe Zack lay in the brush wiping tears away from his eyes as he listened to the killers shouting back and forth. He scowled in fury as he saw the troopers being stripped of their uniforms, and only then did it come to him what was happening. He had to get back to the fort, fast! But he couldn't run ten miles. There was no chance he could get to one of the horses without being seen.

Dimly he realized the only thing he could do was to wait for the train to come in. Then maybe he could alert the train crew. He would get on the engineer's side, on the far side of the tracks away from the water tower. If only he had grabbed his carbine before he fell off his mount! But that was something he couldn't think about now. He had to move into a position where he could contact the engineer, warn him about the slaughter, that he was taking on ten killers, not ten army troopers.

Billy Joe didn't know why the troops had been assigned to the train, but they must be protecting something or someone important. Now nine soldiers were dead, all but him. It was up to him to warn the train people. Billy Joe crept deeper into the heavy brush, then circled the area slowly. He moved up to the edge of the brush well beyond the water tank. In one surge of speed he ran across the cleared right of way and into the woods on the far side of the tracks.

Billy Joe flopped down, tired, but pleased. He had made it so far. The hardest part was over. Now all he had to do was guess where the engine would stop, and throw a rock at the engineer to get his attention. After that it would be easy. He would run up and talk to the engineer, explain it and prove that those bushwhackers were fakes. The real army men on board could disarm the outlaws and take them back to Ft. Ruby, charged with murder. The army would like that, it would have a grand mass hanging party!

Billy Joe Zack lay back in the woods now

and shivered. He had never been in a fight with Indians, never shot at a man before. Now he knew he never should have left Philadelphia. He should have stayed right there and married Wanda Sue, the way she wanted him to. Then their baby would have a real father, and Billy Joe would be working in the shoe store waiting for a chance to become an apprentice to a master printer.

The small trooper sighed. Instead, maybe it was fate that sent him here to help save this train and the important men who must be on board. Maybe even the President himself! He smiled in the darkness. The more Billy Joe Zack thought of it, the more he knew it was fate that had brought him to this spot, to do something really important. He listened and far down the tracks he thought he could hear the sounds of the train approaching.

Jim Steel hung out from the first passenger car as the train slowed. The conductor had told him the Ft. Ruby siding was coming up and he had watched for the water tower. The train began slowing before Jim saw the wooden tower, then he spotted it in the moonlight and a ragged line of troopers waiting on the twenty foot long loading platform made of new raw lumber that had been creosoted black. The train wheezed to a stop, and Sgt. Southdown stepped onto the platform and spoke to the sergeant who stood in front of his men.

"Sgt. Bradley here, Sergeant," the soldier waiting said as the other trooper came up.

"Evening, I'm Sgt. Southdown. You have your orders?"

"Right, Southdown. We got to mollycoddle this big train here all the way to Denver. No problem. We can take care of her. Where they have us quartered?"

"This car, Bradley, it's all yours. You leave us some mounts to ride back to the fort?"

"Right, at the hitching rail. We're short one man, came down with a case of mumps. But we brought you an extra horse for your man. Only trouble was he broke a leg and we had to shoot him. You're one mount short."

"We'll get by. None of us have been to Ft. Ruby. Where the hell is the place?"

"About ten miles straight down the stage road. Can't miss it."

He turned. "All right, men. Get on board the first car. Move lively now."

The masquerading soldiers filed on board the train, then the eight real troopers came off and lined up on the platform. They took off the body of the dead soldier as well.

Then Southdown waited.

"My orders were to wait for the train to leave," Southdown said as his men began to squirm. "Just hold steady."

Brad Smith took his men on board, then stepped to the other side of the coupled cars and looked up the tracks. He saw movement along the right of way, stepped off the train and walked beside the car, his army carbine at the ready. Smith checked and the weapon was loaded and ready.

Smith saw movement again, a man at the edge of the brush. He watched in the moonlight until he was sure, a blue shirt and stovepipe army boots. Then he lifted the Springfield carbine and fired twice. The small cavalryman jolted backwards into the brush. Almost at once a tall, lean man with a .45 pistol trained on Smith came out of the last passenger car.

"What's going on?" Jim Steel asked when he saw the sergeant, the gun not wavering from its aim.

"Thought I saw a deer out there. Been a long time since my men had fresh meat. I thought a little venison would taste good to the whole crew and passengers. But afraid I missed him in the dark. Sorry." He held out his hand. "Sgt. Bradley, cavalry."

"I'm Jim Steel, the ramrod on this outfit.

You might say I'm the general here. You take your orders from me. I want that clear right now. So get back on board so we can get out of here as soon as they finish watering."

"Yes, sir!" Brad said and jumped up the train steps.

Fifty yards ahead and half that far from the train's engine, Private Billy Joe Zack struggled to pull one hand forward. He dug his fingers into the soft earth and slid his body three inches toward the train. Zack pushed his right arm out again, digging into the loose soil then levered himself forward.

There was nothing left in his chest. The bullet had torn through everything and he couldn't even talk. He could see and hear, he knew the train was still taking on water. But how could he warn them now?

"Got to warn the engineer!" Billy Joe Zack said, only there was no sound coming from his mouth. His legs wouldn't work at all now. The first shot had bored through his chest, disconnecting all the wires to his legs. They wouldn't do anything he told them. The second shot had smashed into his right arm and went on through into his side. His belly hurt, the round must have angled downward. He hurt like hell.

For a moment he couldn't see. Billy Joe shook his head and his vision cleared. He called out, but the words strangled on blood that surged into his throat. He tried to spit the blood out, but couldn't.

Billy Joe stretched out his arm, dug in his fingers and dragged himself another three inches forward. It was a long way, such a long way to the tracks. But the big black engine still sat there, hissing softly. The huge steel wheels were motionless. Still twenty yards to the tracks. If it were only daylight the engineer could see him. Billy Joe rested. He saw a civilian working on the spout, getting the water into the tank. The water stop must be almost over. Billy Joe knew he had to get there.

Again his arm went out, his fingers caught into the ground and he pulled forward. Now his ears buzzed, and his right arm screamed in agony. He hurt all over. Billy Joe knew he could still do it. Sometimes the trains waited here a half hour.

Then the man on top swung back into the train cab and Billy Joe saw a second man look out the window and stare back down the tracks. It was the engineer.

"Look at me!" Billy Joe screamed without making a sound.

Far back Billy Joe could see a white lantern swing three times, then the big engine's wheels rumbled as the power came too quickly and the drive wheels spun on the slick rails. The next time the power went smoothly to the drive wheels and the long train slowly began to move. Barely moving at first, then faster and faster.

Billy Joe Zack reached out and pulled forward another three inches. He saw the last car roll by and he couldn't stop it. He had to stop the train, to warn them!

Tears splashed his cheeks. Those poor people. They were in the hands of killers, nine killers all ruthless and with army weapons!

He reached out once more and pulled forward. He had to keep working, had to keep moving toward the tracks.

Billy Joe didn't realize it, but more than three hours had passed since the train had left. At last he felt his fingers touch the steel rail of the Union Pacific line. A soft smile came over his pain seared face. He had made it! He had warned them! He had reached the ultimate, the steel rail that connected him directly in an unbroken line with the train. The people were saved! Then, with his fingers gripping the shining steel rail, Billy Joe Zack breathed his last and sighed gently, sure that he had fulfilled his fate and warned the people on the train. The small cavalryman sighed once and joined his nine comrades in arms in the next world.

On board the train, Jim Steel had taken an instant dislike to the tall, redheaded Sgt. Bradley. Jim had lined up the new troopers in their car and stared at them.

"You men are under my specific command by order of the federal government. Just think of me as having an army general's star on my shoulder. Your job is to be a military guard on this civilian train. You'll take any orders I give and carry them out. I spent some time in the army myself and left with the rank of captain, so don't think you can fool me.

"Your job is to safeguard this entire train. If we stop, you will guard the couplings between all cars and guard the engine. While the train is moving four of you will be on guard duty on the tops of the four cars, and you'll be up there to look for trouble, any kind of trouble. Are there any questions?"

There were none. Jim thought the men were the poorest soldiers he had seen in a long time.

"Sargeant, I want you to post those four men on the roofs of the two passenger cars, the baggage car and the box car at once."

"Yes, sir," Sgt. Bradley said and sent four of his men on their way to stand guard.

"Now, Sergeant, I want your two best men. They'll be on guard duty in the baggage car. We've had some trouble back there and I don't want any more. Your men are to be armed with carbines and pistols. Send them along with me now."

"Right, Captain. Marshall, Windlown, you two. Follow the captain here to the rear. You're on guard duty in the baggage car."

Jim led the men into the next passenger car. Mandy stopped him.

"Is everything all right, Jim?" she asked, her bright eyes sparking with interest.

"As good as we can hope for right now," Jim said and kept on going. At the baggage car Jim paused and called loudly.

"Hey, you guards inside the baggage car. This is Jim Steel. Hold your fire and open up. We're coming in."

Jim watched as the civilian guards inside pulled the first trunk down, then the second. When the civilians saw it was Jim and two army men, they lowered their pistols and grinned.

"Damn, it's about time you relieved us," one said. "These the new soldier boys we got helping us?"

"Right. You can come out and catch some sleep." The civilians stepped over the last trunk wedged in the doorway and went into the passenger car. Jim led the two soldiers over the trunk into the long mail baggage car.

"This is the baggage and mail car," Jim said. "It's got a big safe over there and the mail rack back there. Somebody tried to blow the door off a few miles back. As of now, nobody comes in here unless I say so. When I come in it's just like I did this time. You savvy?"

The soldiers both nodded. One of the men stood on each side of Jim.

"Anything else? Any questions you have?" Jim looked from one of the men to the other and when he looked back at the first, a .44 sixgun muzzle pushed into his ribs. It was cocked and a finger was on the trigger.

"Yeah, tin horn captain, sir. How quick do you want to die?"

Both men laughed as if they had played the funniest trick anyone ever thought of.

Jim squeezed his eyes into a frown. "I should have known. No wonder you look like such bad soldiers. Your uniforms don't even fit. You bushwhacked the real soldiers, right?"

"You talk too damn much, Steel. Move over by the side door there," the biggest of the men said. He reached down and pulled out Jim's revolver. The second soldier chuckled and unlocked the sliding side door used for loading and pushed it wide open. Wind rushed into the car, the rail sounds came much louder and Jim could see night lighted trees rushing past.

"Now, Captain, your little game is over. You just wander over there in front of the big door so I can blow you right out of the car with some nudges from these .44 slugs. Come on, walk over there."

Jim didn't move. Now he felt the pressure increase on the .44 and he took a step away from the gun.

"Keep going, you son-of-a-bitch. I don't want to have to lug your big carcass that far to pitch it out."

"All of you are ringers, right?" Jim asked.

"Hell yes, all nine of us. Teddy bought a slug in the head when we talked the army boys out of their pretty blue uniforms. Brad said we could whip them bastards, and it was no contest. Mowed the suckers down. Now move it, Steel. Another six steps or I'll start shooting at your knees and work up until I find something vital, you want it that way?"

Jim shook his head. He saw no way out, no way at all. He could rush the man, hope the bullets missed his heart or head. Jim knew he'd take at least two slugs. The chance of his coming out alive that way were slim. But at least it was some chance.

Backing up to that open door was sudden death, Jim knew that. There was no big decision to make. Jim knew he had to rush the big man, somehow hope that he could deflect the gun before it killed him. Jim saw the gunman lift the .44 and aim it at Jim's chest. He sucked up his stomach ready for his one last, desperate charge.

But before Jim could move a shot blasted through the confines of the baggage car.

CHAPTER 13

Jim heard the shot blast in the baggage car and wondered for a split second if this were death; but he didn't hurt anywhere. He saw the gunman in front of him lean to one side, stagger, and noticed the surprised look on the man's face, then the killer in his blue uniform who had been threatening Jim, stumbled forward.

Jim half caught the man, stripped the six-gun from his relaxed hand and swung the weapon to cover the second fake soldier by the big sliding door.

"Don't try for the hogsleg," Jim barked. The smaller man let his hand slide slowly to his side, away from the gun butt. The bushwhacker in front of Jim slumped to the floor, one hand trying to stem the flow of blood at his side.

Jim looked toward the door, saw the curl of black powder smoke from the muzzle of a derringer that showed, resting on top of the steamer trunk. Jim had a strange feeling as he noticed the delicate arm holding the gun. The rest of the person was hidden in the darkness.

Jim glanced back at the bushwhacker by the door, then at the derringer. "Come out of there, whoever you are," Jim commanded.

Mandy Martindale stepped out of the shadows in front of the car. Jim had not ordered the men to close up the doorway yet when they captured him.

"Mandy!" Jim said, his hunch proving true. "Lady, you sure do show up at important times!" Jim sent a threatening glance back at the gunman at the door who had edged his hand up his leg again.

Mandy's face was white, her eyes stared straight ahead. Jim wasn't sure that she heard what he said. Jim looked back at the gunman again. The man had just cleared leather with his gun and it was coming up to aim at Jim. Jim shot twice. The twin .45 reports blasted into the silence of the baggage car, stunning ear drums with the battering noise, as the two slugs tore into the blue blouse of the masquerading soldier. The first bullet cut his aorta in half, and the second pulverized the man's spinal column dropping him dead to the floor.

Jim ran to Mandy and caught her just

before she fell. He moved her back to the trunk and sat her down, put his arm around her and pillowed her head against his shoulder.

Her white face turned up toward him, her soft brown eyes now dull, her jaw slack, lips slightly parted. She automatically brushed long brown hair from her face and stared at Jim.

"I . . . I actually shot that man."

"Yes, Mandy."

"Is he . . . is he . . . hurt badly?"

Jim looked at the closer of the two men on the floor. The blue shifted man hadn't moved since he stumbled and fell. Jim guessed the .45 derringer round had entered his side from a low angle and traveled upward into his heart or lungs.

"Don't worry about the man. The important thing is that you just saved my life! You know he was about to kill me. That's why you shot. You saved my life, Mandy Martindale, and I thank you."

She blinked, her gaze still on the other man. "Is he hurt badly?" she asked.

"Yes, but I can't tell how badly from here."

"Would you . . . would you go . . ."

Jim moved away from her after deciding she wouldn't fall over, and checked the bushwhacker in the soldier's uniform. Jim put his finger to the neck to test the large carotid artery. There was no sign of a heart beat. Jim touched the temple artery, but again found no pulse. Jim straightened and walked back to the girl, sat on the steamer trunk beside her and put his arms around her.

"The man is in no pain, Mandy. No pain at all. He's dead."

Mandy gasped, then the tears came. He held her tightly as her face pushed hard into his chest. She wailed and cried as the tears washed down her cheeks. He let her cry. The wind whipped in the open side door and out the blown off end door. He knew he should get the openings closed and barricaded. There were still eight desperate killers on board and they were trying for the gold.

Jim bent and wiped away her tears as Mandy stopped sobbing. He let her use his kerchief to dry her eyes, then kissed each eye carefully, and at last he kissed her still trembling lips. She responded hungrily and for a moment she clung to him so he thought she might never let go. Then she eased back and he kissed her lips lightly again.

"You just saved my life, Mandy. I'll never forget that. Now, we have work to do. We'll cry and kiss again later. But right now we have to survive. All right?"

She nodded. He took a .45 round from his belt and reloaded the fired barrel on her derringer, then watched when she put it in its pocket in her skirt.

He went to the first man, drug him to the side door of the baggage car and rolled him out into the night.

Mandy gasped.

"We really can't leave them in here, can we?" Jim asked. "Especially since we're going to invite some more of their friends in." Jim threw out the second dead ambusher after prying the sixgun from his death grip. Then Jim came back and put his arms around Mandy.

"I want you to do something for me. Can you do that?"

"I'll try."

"You can't cry if you do it."

"I've had my cry. It isn't every day that I kill a man."

"I realize that. We'll try not to kill any more of them, and you can help. I want you to go back to the passenger car and send in one of our civilian guards, one of the men from the mine. Send him back quickly, and pick the first one you recognize. Can you do that? Then stay in your seat in the car and wait for me."

She nodded, wiped her eyes once more and swung over the steamer trunk and to the outside doorway of the car.

Jim moved quickly, spreading a mail sack over the blood near the center of the car where the first man had died. Then he closed the side loading door, locked it, and made everything as normal as he could.

The guard was there in a moment. He looked around quickly.

"Where are the soldiers?"

"On the roof," Jim said easily. "We need two more of the blue shirts back here. Can you go to the sergeant in the second car up and tell him I said to send two men back with you?"

"Sure."

"And on your way up there, send me two of our mine guards, any two that look rested. Get them back here quickly."

"Right." The man vaulted the trunk and left.

The two civilians came first, and Jim had them go to the far end of the car into the shadows. He explained what would be happening and the men grinned and checked the rounds in their sixguns. They both were well back in the shadows and hard to see.

Jim stood in the mail sorting area waiting.

The two soldiers who came in looked at the blasted off door and laughed. Then they saw Jim and sobered.

"Hey, Captain, what can we do for you?" one asked.

"First you can stand at attention and let me look at your weapons. You're damn sloppy soldiers, and I've got to know if your side arms are in working order."

"Yes, sir. I guarantee that they work," the other soldier said grinning.

Jim slid his own .45 out of the holster so quickly both the other men frowned in surprise.

"Just hold it right there," Jim said, the .45 covering both men without seeming to. "I don't want to kill either one of you if I don't have to, although you both deserve it and I will gladly shoot you dead if it comes to that. Get their guns, boys."

The killers now looked scared. They glanced at Jim's weapon, then at the two men who came out of the shadows with their sixguns aimed at them. Neither bushwhacker made a move. The guards pulled the weapons from the fake soldiers and pushed the men toward the side door. One civilian rolled the door open and Jim stared at the killers for a moment.

"I should shoot you and throw you off the

train," Jim said. "But I'll give you a choice. You can go out the door with lead in your bellies or without any."

The men looked at each other and shrugged. "Without," one of them said. "Can we pick a soft spot to land?"

"Did you give those ten troopers a chance to pick their spot?" Jim waited a second, then fired a shot past the men and out the door. "Jump, right now," Jim spat at them.

Both went out the door without hesitation and without looking back.

"Four down," Jim said. "Six to go. The only problem is we don't want to turn this train into a battlefield. Not with all those civilians in the way. We've got to do it carefully, and quietly." Jim looked at the two mine guards. "You guys stay in here. When I go out close up the door with those trunks. Jam them in tight. Then roll shut the side door and lock it. Don't let anyone in here but me. And keep everything just as it is. I'm going to take a short guided tour."

Jim went through the connecting doors and sat down beside Mandy. The tears were gone, but she was brittle-bright, her nerves stretched thin and tight but not yet broken. Jim put his arm around her shoulders and she snuggled against him, her eyes blinking rapidly.

"Damnit, I won't cry again!" she said softly but with a tense strained intensity. "Would you please kiss me or say something nice to me so I don't go stark raving mad?"

He bent and kissed her cheek. "Better than that, I'll give you a job to do, pretty girl. You've seen Forrest Billings, the saloon keeper in Sacramento?"

"Yes, I've seen him. He was on the coach and you handcuffed him but he got away from the next car."

"He's still on the train. He's the one responsible for all of our problems, both inside and outside the train. He's still here so he must be disguised somehow. Your job is to find him. I have to get rid of the rest of these phoney soldiers. Four down and six yet to go. We let the other two jump out the door, so don't waste any tears on them. I want that sergeant all tied up and put in a sack to deliver to the army for the deaths of those ten troopers. The army people will draw and quarter him if they get the chance."

She nodded and turned looking back up the coach.

"I think I'll pay some social calls on my traveling neighbors. I really haven't been very neighborly." She smiled and he shook his head and waited. She smiled again and this time the dimples punched into both cheeks. He lifted his hand and let her slide past him into the aisle.

Jim moved forward quietly. He had spotted one of the soldiers talking with a civilian. But as Jim approached the soldier bent and talked with two more passengers, then returned to the next coach. By the time Jim got into the soldier's car, he realized the man talking had been the redheaded sergeant, and now he was with the only other blue shirt in the coach. Bradley turned as Jim came up.

"You really need four of my men to guard the baggage car?" Sgt. Bradley asked.

"Yes Sergeant, and I don't stand for insubordination. And I don't want you mixing with the paying passengers. The customers are nervous enough with all the problems we've been having without you telling them some wild Indian raid stories."

"I was only trying to find out the time of day. It seems none of these people have watches." He looked up at Jim with a slight frown. "And I'm not so sure you have total authority here. My captain said there would be a man on board with military orders for us, written orders. You don't seem to have any paper that says what you or we are supposed to be doing."

Jim knew the man was deliberately provoking him. He held onto his temper with an effort. "I assure you I have the authority. What you should be worrying about is how you're going to keep your stripes when this project is over. I'm restricting you and your off-duty men to this car. Is that understood? I'll personally escort the guards from their posts to this car. You keep them in here and keep them quiet."

Jim turned and walked out of the car without looking back. In the passenger coach he found one of the mine guards he remembered, a tall kid named Walt.

"Start at the baggage car, Walt, and go to the roof of the next four cars and tell the soldier guards that they will be relieved in about fifteen minutes. We'll be taking the guards down and not put up any new ones. When you get them all told, come back to the baggage car and meet me."

Walt nodded and went to the rear car at once.

Jim sat in the coach watching. There couldn't be more than about twenty paying passengers. Surely one of them had to be the gambler, Forrest Billings. But which one? He couldn't search each person, disrobe them all, pull at fake whiskers.

Walt came through on his way to tell the

next roof guard. He was back three or four minutes later.

"Told them all, Mr. Steel," Walt said. Jim nodded and waved for Walt to follow him and they went back to the connection between the baggage and the passenger cars.

"Climb up and tell him it's time to come down," Jim told Walt. "Tell him to pass down his carbine first so he doesn't drop it."

Walt went up three rungs on the ladder and yelled at the guard who passed down his carbine, and then Walt jumped back to the platform between the cars. The bushwhacker was on the last rung when Jim leaned out and tapped his knuckles on the steel rung with a revolver.

"That's far enough, killer. I'll take that .44 of yours so you don't get any foolish ideas. We know all about the troopers you slaughtered. You want a bullet in you as you go off the side, or you want to jump free and easy?"

The face that looked at Jim was surprised, then frightened. The man was about twenty-five and slender with a mustache.

"Jump? I'll kill myself. We're on a bridge. It's fifty feet to the ground!"

"I hope you find a soft spot to land. You've got five seconds, then I'm shooting you off

those rungs. Four . . . three . . . two . . ."
The wild-eyed bushwhacker jumped, then
he screamed and his voice was slashed away
in the wind of the train and the noise of the
wheels.

"Five down, five to go," Jim said. They
worked up to the second passenger car and
forced each of the other two men to jump,
then there were only three of the fake troopers left: the guard on top of the box car just
beyond the passenger car, and the two men
inside the number one passenger coach.

"We'll save both of them in the coach for
the army," Jim said. He nodded to Walt. "We
go in with our guns out, disarm these two
and tie them up. Then we get the conductor
with his key and put the pair in the morgue
with the other bodies. We'll get the last roof
man after that." Jim was angry now. "I
almost hope they try to shoot their way out."

Jim went in first through the connecting
door into the soldier's car, his .45 in front
of him, covering both men who were playing a game of cards.

"On your feet, nice and easy like," Jim
said. He felt Walt backing him up. "Stand
slow and put your hands on top of your
heads, or you'll be eating lead for supper,"
Jim said.

The two men stood carefully, hands soon

laced on top of their heads. The sergeant's scowl was complete.

"Go get their guns, Walt," Jim said.

Just as Walt blocked Jim's view of the men, Bradley yelled, and a man jumped up from the far end of the car and began shooting. Jim lunged for a seat back and got off two shots as he moved. The firing from the far end of the coach stopped, and Jim heard Walt get off one shot, then saw Walt bring his .45 down hard on the head of the second bushwacker.

When Jim stood, the sergeant lay with blood streaming from his head. Half his face had been splattered with a .45 round. The second man lay on the floor, holding his battered face with his hands.

Jim ran to the other end of the car, his .45 ready. But the last of the fake soldiers lay crumpled over his sixgun, a slug in his chest. He was dead by the time Jim got there.

"Throw the two dead ones off the train," Jim told Walt. "I'm going to find the conductor."

The trainman sat in the back seat of the civilian's coach, eating a sandwich. He grumbled about being disturbed, but Jim prodded him back to the next coach to open the locked room where the bodies lay. Walt had cleaned the blood from the last of the fake soldiers and tied his hands and feet securely. Jim and Walt lay the live bushwacker on the floor in the small morgue room, that had been promoted to jail. There was no window, no possible way to escape.

"You mean that man's still alive and you're going to lock him up in there with all those corpses?" the conductor asked. "My God, man, that's inhuman!"

"Don't reckon the dead ones will hurt him any," Jim said. "Besides, him and his buddies shot down ten regular army men in cold blood from ambush, stole their uniforms and weapons and came on board to kill all of us and take the gold. You think that's human? Lock the damn door and give me the key."

The conductor did as he was told.

"Now, I'm going to find that madman Forrest Billings," Jim said. "No excuses, no alibis. If we want this train to get to Denver, we've got to find Billings, and right away!"

CHAPTER 14

Jim Steel walked to the second passenger coach with determination but no set plan how he was going to do his job of ferreting out Billings. The gambler was still there somewhere, and on the train, Jim was sure.

First, the low level approach. He caught Mandy's glance as she left the two women halfway down the gas-lit car.

"Find anyone who could be Billings?" Jim asked her.

Soft brown eyes told him she hadn't. "Not a prayer. I've been talking to the women and watching the men. I can't figure out how any of these men could possibly be the tall, thin-faced gambler. Most of these men are too short, or too old."

"I've looked them over a dozen times," Jim said. "I found the same problem. But he's here, he has to be here. And I've checked every compartment in the train. There just is no place a man can hide. So how do we find him, Mandy?"

She brought her lips together in a firm, determined line, but at last she looked up and shook her head.

"All right, we do it the hard way." He stood, whistled shrilly through his fingers, and everyone looked at him.

"Ladies and gentleman. As you know we've been having some problems on this train ride. One man has been causing all of that trouble and he's on board the train right now. In fact, that man is in the passenger car right now. What we've got to do is find him. His name is Forrest Billings and he's a saloon owner from Sacramento. He's also a killer, a scoundrel, a conspirator, and the man who has planned to kill us all if he has to. He would gladly slaughter everyone on this train if he could steal the fortune in the baggage car. Now, I'd like you people here to help me find him.

"First, I'd like all of the guards from the Lucky Seven mine to move to the far end of the coach. All of the mine men, whether you came on as a guard or a passenger."

He paused and leaned down to Mandy. "You go back there and check them. See if you can find one of them who doesn't belong or see if any of them might be Forrest Billings in disguise."

She nodded, stood and went to the end of the car where the men had gathered.

Jim looked at those left, about twenty persons.

"Now, we'll play Quaker for a minute. I want all of the women to move to the right hand seats, and all the men to move to the left hand side. This won't take but a few moments, then you can sit anywhere you want to again. My right please. I hear the seats are softer on the right hand side."

That brought a few nervous laughs, but the women and men began to move and as they did Jim watched, but he saw no one who looked nervous or uncomfortable. He wondered if Billings might have an accomplice on board, a woman even. He doubted it.

Jim moved along the rows, looking at the men who now sat on the left side. There were nine in all.

"Gentlemen, would you stand for me please? The person I'm looking for is tall, so that lets most of you out at once. Just stand for a comparison, please." The men grumbled a bit but they all stood. Jim frowned. Everyone of them was far too short to be Billings except the older man Jim had seen before. There was no chance the tall, older man with the puffy face and sparse white beard could be Billings in disguise. Jim scowled this time.

"Gentlemen, are any of you armed?"

There was an agitating murmuring by some of the nine. Then the one nearest to Jim put it into words.

"Well, mister. I don't exactly know who you are, but if none of us is the killer you're looking for, looks like we got a right to hold onto our weapons to defend ourselves, if we do have any."

"Yes, good point. The thought did occur to me. I thank you all for your cooperation. Thank you." They sat down. Jim walked half way up the car and looked at the women's side. He was undecided. It was the only option he had left.

"Ladies, I know it's probably a waste of time, but I'd like to ask you to stand. Would you mind? Then I'll tell each of you how pretty you are, and we'll get on down the tracks toward Denver. We should also be able to turn down the lights so all of you can have some sleep as well. Please, ladies, just stand where you are."

Some did at once. There were twelve of them. Three hesitated, then at last stood. None of the women was tall enough to matter. None could be Billings in disguise.

Then Jim saw a woman leaning against

the window, her eyes closed, breathing long and deep.

"I think we have one sleeping already," Mandy said. She moved into the seat beside the sleeping woman and touched her lightly on the shoulder. Nothing happened. The woman wore an old hat and veil and a worn brown coat. Mandy pushed the woman's shoulder, shaking her slightly.

So quickly Mandy couldn't explain it, the woman grabbed Mandy's wrist and spun her around twisting Mandy's arm behind her back. The woman stood and a .44 caliber sixgun came up in her right hand. As she stood the overhead rack caught at her hair and a long brown wig came off and hung on the rack.

The woman was really a man in a dress. The thin face of Forrest Billings glared at them.

"Don't nobody move," Billings roared. "You do and this girl gets shot full of holes. I'm not joking. One more corpse makes no difference to me."

Jim had seen the first movement of the sleeping woman, and he guessed who she had to be, so he ducked completely out of sight behind a seat and drew his revolver. There would be no chance to use the weapon in the car. By hiding now he could prevent a gunfight in the coach, and perhaps have an advantage later.

Billings looked around. "Where's that damned Jim Steel? I heard him just a minute ago." Billings looked at each face, then the big man in the woman's flowing green dress pushed Mandy out to the aisle.

"You mine guards drop your weapons, right now. Lay them on the floor. Right now or your boss's daughter gets a bullet in her spine. Now, damnit!"

The guards put their rifles and pistols on the floor. Billings backed toward the baggage car end of the coach. The guards were at the other end. He knew Steel was there somewhere, but he couldn't waste time hunting for him.

Billings crouched behind the small girl, pulling her backwards with him. He checked some of the seats as he passed, but didn't see Steel.

At the coach door, he opened it and backed through pulling Mandy with him into the small area between the cars.

Billings pointed to the rungs leading to the top of the car.

"Up you go, climb to the top of the car, right now!"

"I can't."

"You can, you ride a horse, you're a

regular tomboy. Now get up there!" He prodded her with the gun. She remembered the derringer in her pocket but there was no time now. Gingerly she caught the iron rungs of the ladder and climbed up and looked over the top of the car. It was flat, but swaying and bouncing. For a moment she knew she would fall off. Then Billings yelled at her and she pushed over the top and sat down, spreading her legs so she wouldn't roll off.

It seemed much darker up here, with the cool evening air rushing past, and the towering trees along the right of the way standing like stones in a giant's graveyard.

The derringer? She could shoot Billings as he climbed up the ladder. But could she pull the trigger again? Could she do that even knowing what Billings had done? She didn't think she could. Not yet. A moment later she heard a shot below, then boots sounded on the ladder rungs.

Billings came over the top of the car in a rush, his women's dress discarded, and wearing a dark shirt and pants she had seen him in before. She saw him plainly in the dark, and some smoke still came from the end of his sixgun. He ran toward her, hesitated, then stepped around her and charged quickly along the top of the swaying car and into the blackness ahead. Mandy crawled to the end of the car and looked down.

"Jim! Jim!" she called.

"Yes? Mandy?"

"He's gone. He's running down the top of the next car toward the engine!"

Jim Steel surged up the ladder past Mandy to the roof and then rushed hard after the man ahead. Jim snapped a shot at Billings, saw the flash as a weapon fired in the dark in reply, then Jim ran full speed, jumped to the second passenger car, and paused. Suddenly he dropped flat on top of the car.

A trap. Billings would be on the ladder at the end of the passenger car waiting for Jim to get closer. The first shot from Billings came, hitting the steel top of the roof three feet from Jim, whining away into the trees.

Jim now crawled silently, watching the top of the end of the car. He could see little. Jim moved faster, then waited, but nothing happened. There was nowhere for Billings to go. The freight car lay ahead. It was locked and sealed. The door to the passenger car on this end was locked. Billings was trapped.

The second shot from Billings came a moment later from the left hand side of the car. Jim did not return the fire. That was four rounds the gambler had used. But did he have five or six rounds in his weapon, and had he reloaded? Jim didn't know.

"Give it up, Billings, that was your last round. It's like shooting fish in a barrel now for me." The moment Jim said it he rolled to the other side of the car. A bullet slapped the steel top a second after Jim vacated the spot.

Jim edged forward on his hands and knees. He was still twenty feet from the end of the car when Billings reared up, the weapon held with two hands now, his eyes straining into the darkness. Both men fired at the same time. Jim felt the slug tear a groove along his right forearm, and the six-gun he held spun away from him as his hand jerked backwards.

Jim's round hit Billings's revolver on the cylinder, slamming it out of Billings's hand and numbing his whole arm. Jim was up and running forward, stomping at the man's hands where they held the top of the roof, kicking at Billings's head and shoulders.

Billings caught Jim's foot with both hands and twisted, shoving Jim backwards, dumping Jim to his hands and knees on the roof. It gave Billings time to leap over the end of the car and come at Jim who had time only to scramble up to meet him. In the splintered moonlight through the shadow of tall trees, Jim saw the glint of the knife Billings held. The blade came one way and Jim kicked high, grazing the knife arm. They worked backward on the car top.

Jim could see his revolver lying on top of the roof, but he was being forced away from it. He kicked again, his boot connecting solidly with Billings's knee, staggering him. But there was no chance for Jim to run and get the weapon or disarm Billings.

They moved again, back down the car top as Jim gave way before the flashing six-inch blade. Neither man spoke, eyes gleaming in the soft moonlight, breath coming faster. Each man knew he was in a battle to the death.

Then Jim stumbled over a vent tube and fell backwards. Billings drove in, the knife held low to ram into Jim's heart. But Jim's feet came up, kicking hard, connected with Billings's right wrist, and the knife skittered toward the side of the roof, then slid over the edge and fell away. Jim's second foot drove into Billings's stomach, knocking some of the wind out of him, sending Billings onto the car roof hard to Jim's right. Jim rolled that way, reaching for Billings's head. But the tall man squirmed away and now he was retreating.

Jim drove Billings back toward the end of the coach roof. Whenever Billings slowed, Jim's hard fists slammed into his jaw or his stomach. Once Billings grappled with Jim and they rolled on the swaying roof. They both had to let go of the other to keep from rolling off the edge.

"Give it up, Billings. I'll see that you get a fair trial."

"Sure, an honest rope, I've seen that before. Not me."

Jim caught him with a roundhouse right fist, then kicked at Billings's planted right foot. Jim's hard-toed boot smashed into Billings's ankle bone and the bone broke. Billings's mouth opened and his terrible scream drowned out the train's noise.

Forrest Billings stumbled backwards, his shin bone was shattered, his right foot would not work. He twisted, then screamed again as he tried to step back on his right foot, but instead fell between the railroad cars. Jim ran to the end of the coach and looked down.

Billings hung on the last rung of the ladder on the freight car side. His legs dangled almost touching the rails. He tried to hold on with his still hurting right hand, but his hand came loose from the rung, and Billings dangled by his left hand as his feet searched desperately for a foothold in mid air.

Billings screamed again, looked down at the thundering wheels below him, the rails flashing in the shafts of moonlight as the ties raced past in a blur.

"Help me, Steel!" he shouted. "You've got to help me!"

Before Jim could move to get to the other car, Forrest Billings looked up at Jim and his fingers slipped off the steel rung. He screamed again as he fell. He landed sideways across the shining rail. A cross tie between the rails slammed into Billings's chest twisting his body just before the heavy rail wheels cut his torso in half, the pieces bounding up into the undercarriage where they were pounded, smashed and splattered for half a mile down the right of way before the last of the body of a man known as Forrest Billings fell into the road bed of the Union Pacific Railroad.

CHAPTER 15

Jim lay in the dark on the front edge of the passenger coach roof seeing again the stark, unimaginable terror that filled Forrest Billings's face as Billings knew his fingers were slipping from the rung. The man knew for a few seconds that he was going to die, almost at once, and that there wasn't a thing he or anyone else could do about it or prevent it.

Jim closed his eyes, trying to blot out the face, then as he remembered the dozen or more men who had died because of the greed of Forrest Billings, Jim shunted the image aside, stood and walked slowly back to the end of the first car roof and went down the ladder rungs carefully, glanced at the deadly wheels for a moment, then swung over to the steel platform between the cars. He would never ride a train again without remembering Forrest Billings.

When Jim entered the second passenger car, he saw that the guards and the paying passengers alike had settled down for a try at getting some sleep on the uncomfortable seats.

The railroad hadn't sent any of its plush rolling stock on this run yet. The seats were better than the bare benches some used, but not much. The gas lights in the coach had been turned down to a flicker and Jim saw Mandy rushing up the aisle toward him before he could start to look for her.

She hugged him tightly, pressed her face close to his chest and he heard a contented little sigh. She looked up.

"I've been worried about you. What happened? Tell me all about it. Where is Billings? Are any more of his men still on the train?"

He smiled, saw the worry lines easing on her forehead, and put his arm around her as they walked past the cold, potbellied stove in the middle of the car to her seat near the back. They sat down and she reached out and kissed his lips softly, then snuggled down beside him and looked up.

"Now, tell me what happened."

He gave her the details quickly, glossing over the way Billings died. But he made it plain that Billings had been the last of the conspirators on board the train.

"So now we're safe all the way into Denver. We can relax and try to enjoy the sights?"

Jim shook his head. "Not necessarily. It's my guess that Billings had a series of attacks planned all along the line. If one didn't work out, and the train got past it, like the log on the tracks, then the second plan was carried out. To trigger the plan this train only has to arrive at the location, then the plan goes into operation."

"Like the fire on the tracks and the ambush by the horsemen in the little valley?" Mandy asked.

"Right. So the fact that Billings is dead will not slow the other attacks. He may have two or three more surprises for us up the line. And right now I don't know where we are on the trip, or how much longer we run before we come to a fair-sized little town."

"But we shouldn't have any more trouble tonight?"

"I'm not sure, Mandy. If I were the engineer I'd slow down some at night. That light isn't the best and someone could put a log on the tracks and derail us easily. It all depends what Billings's weird brain figured out when he planned this whole thing."

She didn't seem to hear. "I brought a blanket, and an afghan that I made myself. We could kind of put it over us to keep a little warmer."

He put his arm around her and spread the blanket. She smiled and pushed closer against him.

"I'm so tired I could just die," she said. "One small kiss goodnight and I might be able to sleep for a couple of hours." She reached up to him. When Jim kissed her he found her small mouth open, her tongue darting at his. He held the kiss only for a few seconds, then eased away.

"Hey now, small girl," he said surprised.

She grinned. "That's just a sample, but it may have to hold you until we get to Denver." She caught his hand and held it tightly, then closed her eyes and Mandy was sleeping before Jim had time to think clearly about what she had said, what she had promised. He pulled his hat down over his eyes. He'd go see the engineer the first thing in the morning.

On his way back through the car a few minutes before, Jim had told two guards to have one man stay awake for two hours in each of the cars, then pick replacements, and work on through to daylight. Jim really didn't expect any trouble, but he figured he should have a guard out anyway.

He awoke just before daylight and worked

his way forward, taking two fresh guards with him to relieve the man with the engineer. The rested guards watched the fireman feeding the hungry fire box, understood what was needed and sent the other guards back to the car to go to sleep.

Jim eyed Josh, the fireman pressed into service as engineer.

"How do you stay awake night and day?" Jim asked.

Josh shrugged. "Get used to it on a run. I catch ten to fifteen minute naps sometimes when I know the road is straight and there shouldn't be any problems. I let the fireman ride the throttle. Nothing unusual. Hear you had some more problems back there last night."

Jim told the engineer about the ten fake soldiers, and he shook his head. "Good thing we don't run the railroad like that," Josh said, "or we'd never get anywhere."

Josh glanced ahead. "I figure we got some more trouble coming up. I been worrying it some."

"How's that?" Jim asked.

"If I was going to take out a train to get me some gold, I'd really put the rig down. I'd dump the whole string into a ravine somewhere."

"How?"

"Easy, let the train get half way across a trestle or a bridge and blow tarnation out of the middle of the span and the weight of the string of cars drops the whole train right through the rest of the timbers into the gorge below. Doesn't matter how high. Three hundred feet or thirty feet, off the tracks is a dead train, and most of the people on board are either hurt or dead. Then I'd swing in with about thirty men, dynamite the safe into a pile of scrap and clear out with the gold in saddlebags or on pack horses."

"And all that could be set up before hand, whether Billings is now dead or alive."

"Right. When the train gets to a certain bridge, they blow up the timbers and drop her into a gorge."

Jim stared at the tracks ahead. "Any likely prospects up in front of us here?"

"Plenty," Josh said. "We're in the mountains, we've got mountains most of the way to Denver. Chances every ten to twenty miles to have a bridge or a trestle."

"If you were going to dump it as close to the California end as you could, where would you pick? What trestle near us now?"

The new engineer rubbed his stubbled jaw. "Hell, I don't know. Any one of half a dozen spots. There are four in a row within five or six miles of each other. Climbing from this side, so you don't have a lot of power or speed. But with two charges . . ." He was thinking out loud.

Josh nodded. "Okay, I got them. Three of them coming up in an hour or so. Johnson curve is the first. She's a thirteen-stack high, made of wood, sound as a dollar, only she's on a slight curve and from this side, it's a downgrade. Perfect spot. But a little hard to get to from any town around there. It probably won't be Johnson, but we'll watch it. Slow down, take it easy so if we see she's been blown, we can get the people off."

"Get the passengers off the train? How?" Jim asked.

"Jump them off."

"But we've got women and some old men. None of them have jumped off a train. They'll break their necks."

"Then we put them off at the next flag stop. Got one coming up in another ten, fifteen miles. Little place they can sleep over. If we find no problems, the passengers come through on a train tomorrow, or the next one along."

"Let's do it," Jim said. "But is Johnson Curve this side or the other side of that little town?"

"Timber Junction is on the other side. We

got to pray a little about Johnson curve."

Jim went back and told the conductor what they were going to do about the rest of the trip.

"Unthinkable, rousting passengers off a train. I won't allow it," Conductor Franklin said.

"Then you want to be responsible for jumping all these people off the train if a bridge gets blown up just ahead of us?"

"Bridge . . . oh, my. Who said . . . Yes, I see. With this shipment of gold it could happen. All right. I'll notify the people about a change in schedule, a track repair crew and a layover, something."

Jim told Mandy about the discharge of passengers.

"And you, young lady, will be one of those leaving the train," he said. "No tricks, now please. We can't risk any more lives than we have to. I want only ten guards with me, and they are all volunteers. I just picked them out. The conductor and brakesman are along and the engineer and that's it. The conductor will be telling the people shortly."

"But I want to be with you."

"You don't want to be dead with me. This is my job, so I've got to do it or give up. Everything will probably be all right and the train will sail through, then you can come in on the next train tomorrow. No arguments, we can't afford the time." He stood, looked sternly down at her brown troubled eyes, bent and kissed her cheek, then went back to the engineer.

Twenty minutes later they crept toward Johnson curve trestle at five miles an hour. Jim had not seen anyone on the trestle as they approached it. He had used the binoculars that were in the engine cab.

Josh shrugged at Jim and eased the throttle forward. "So what the hell, we give it a try. If we go down, we go down," Josh said. "I told my old lady I never wanted to live forever."

The fireman rested and the guard with the rifle had his weapon cocked and ready.

The engine came to the edge of the trestle and edged out into space. Only the thin ribbons of steel kept it going in the right direction, and right then Jim distrusted them mightily.

Jim sweated as he watched the trestle from the fireman's side window. He was on the inside of the curve so he could see all of it. There was no one on the long bridge, and he saw no one clinging to the wooden interlocking short beams that built up the bridge.

"Be halfway across in three minutes," Josh

said. "That's the trouble slowing down, takes longer to get across this bitch. They should blow this one in the middle now if they aim to. All they have to do is cut a hole for the engine and the other cars will tag along, roll right into it from behind."

"Thanks for explaining it to me," Jim said. He scanned the tracks ahead. Nothing. He could see nothing ahead that indicated any danger. No long burning fuses to a case of dynamite, no barrel of black powder.

"Halfway," Josh said. "Another two minutes and we've got it whipped." He pushed the throttle ahead and the train picked up speed then as if rushing to get to the other side.

Jim kept his eyes focused on the tracks as far ahead as he could see them, then the rails straightened and they were back on solid land again.

"Scratch one trestle ambush," Josh said. "We could stop at Timber and unload your gold too and you could run it the rest of the way by slow wagon. Pile in some crates of chickens on top of the gold and you'll roll right through."

Jim laughed and asked how far to Timber Junction.

"Another ten minutes, I won't forget to stop."

Jim went back to the coaches and found people getting ready to leave the train. There were a dozen arguments and comments from the passengers, all unfavorable. Jim didn't listen to any of them. He worked his way down the filled aisle to Mandy's seat. She had her picnic basket ready, her small valise all bundled up and the blanket and afghan tied and loaded on top. He nodded and smiled at her, but Mandy would hardly look at him.

"Ridiculous," Mandy said. "I'm as good at jumping off trains as any of those volunteers you picked. Harry Leon, I know he's never jumped off a train before, because this is his very first train ride."

He shushed her and gently pushed her down in the seat and sat beside her.

"Don't give me trouble. I know you could get off the train. But you also could break your leg, or your back or your neck in the process. I don't want you to do that. We might not even have time to jump off but would have to crawl off onto the tracks, maybe with nothing but cool air between the ties over some bridge or on a trestle. Now relax, and take it easy, and get off the train like I told you to and stay happy. I'll see you at the Denver House."

She sighed. He stood and worked his way

along the aisle to the door where the conductor was about to open up. The train jolted to a stop and they had arrived safely at Timber Junction.

The door opened, the step went down and Jim watched as Mandy stepped off the train and stood with the others, watching the train, not concerned with the dozen stores and houses behind them. Mandy waved, then turned and he lost her in the crowd.

Jim jumped to the ground and ran along the station platform to the engine.

"Thought I'd come in the normal way for a change," Jim said. Josh got a quick all clear wave from the conductor, who looked longingly at the village, then swung back on the last passenger car as the train pulled out.

Jim had given the guards, the brakeman and conductor strict orders about jumping. They were to jump if they even thought the train was in danger of derailing or crashing through a bridge. The men in the baggage compartment car were to ride with the side door open. Josh said there would be three short blasts on the train whistle if the train was to be abandoned. Three short blasts meant get off the rig in a rush.

"I hope this is all precaution we don't have to follow through on," Jim said.

Josh shook his head. "Afraid not. Whoever

set this up had all the ideas worked out ahead of time. He'd think of this one, as the last chance for the gold. One final way to kill a train and win the golden prize. All we have to decide is which bridge he picked."

"What's your guess? Which is nearest to a town where they could get horses and wagons to haul the gold?"

"I'd guess through here it would be Pine Valley, about twenty-odd miles up the line. The bridge there is at least a hundred feet over Pine Creek. It's on a straight run through there, so we could see the middle of it blow from half a mile back and come to a stop."

"So if they try to blow that one, they have to cut a short fuse and blow it just as we get there," Jim said.

They worried the run for the next half hour, went over two more possible bridges. Again they slowed and edged out, then sped up going on across. There was no trouble at either one.

Jim stood on the engine tender now, the field glasses glued to his eyes. A half a mile ahead he could see little. As the train moved closer to the next trestle, Jim watched harder. He saw Josh wave out of the engine cab: the trestle at Pine Valley was just ahead of them.

Jim strained his eyes as he watched. It was a mile away yet. Then the tracks straightened and he saw the valley between the trees. He watched closely. Near the far side of the bridge he saw something. Jim wiped his eyes and looked again. Then he was sure. Two men had left the center of the bridge and had run pell-mell for the other side. Jim crawled down to the cab.

"Two of them. Two men just ran off the far side of the bridge. I couldn't see much else."

At once Josh began slowing the train. "Down grade now, I couldn't set the brakes and get it stopped in time if they blew it. Best I can hope for is slow her down."

Both Jim and Josh hung out the windows searching the roadway ahead. They were a hundred yards from the edge of the trestle now.

Then fifty yards out on the wooden trestle they saw and heard the explosion. Jim guessed it was five cases of dynamite that went off, mushrooming up in front of them, shattering rail timbers into kindling wood, bending the heavy rails, curving them back like two giant spaghetti.

Josh hit the whistle and even before the third note sounded, Jim saw men jumping off the train. Then he stared in surprise as a woman jumped off. It had to be Mandy with one bag in each hand. He made sure the two guards left the engine, then he jumped. He carried only his rifle and a belt full of ammunition.

Jim tried to spin as he hit, but he tumbled head over boots, rolling down the ten-foot embankment, stopping in a ditch filled with soft green grass and wildflowers. Jim stood and ran up to the tracks, chasing the train. The brakes were on now, squealing steel against steel, showing sparks. But there wasn't enough room to stop. He saw Josh jump off at the last moment before the train went onto the trestle.

Then the short train slid another fifty yards to the ruptured trestle. The engine hit the curved back rails, mashing them down, plunging over the end into the hole, smashing downward through the lower supports, blasting the timbers like matchsticks, at last spinning to one side and splashing into the small creek with a crashing roar. It pulled the tender and freight car with it, but snapped off the coupling and left the first passenger car rolling along slowly forward. At that point hand brakes might have stopped it.

But without brakes the passenger car rolled faster and faster, then tilted downward and smashed through another ten feet of the crumbling trestle as it collapsed and the second passenger car and baggage car dropped into the gorge on top of the other cars.

The screeching and tearing of metal was something Jim had never heard before, and never wanted to listen to again. He saw Mandy then, down the right of way, and he left the tracks and ran to her, caught her in his arms and hugged her, swinging her around in a circle twice. Then he kissed her and put her down.

"I'm glad you didn't break your silly head, or an arm. Now come on, and keep low, we don't want anyone on the other side to see us if we can help it."

He saw three of the mine guards and waved them to come with him. All were uninjured and had their rifles. Then they gathered up six more guards. The tenth man had broken a leg when he hit a tree as he rolled down the bank after landing.

They knew where he was and would come back for him. The little squad trooped along the right of way to the edge of the gorge and looked down through a fringe of brush and trees.

The rail cars were splayed out like cordwood thrown down in anger. The engine still steamed where it had fallen into the shallow stream. The baggage car had smashed into the last passenger coach and broken in half. Jim wondered which end held the safe and the half million dollars worth of pure gold.

"Let's keep out of sight and be quiet," Jim said. "If I don't miss my guess someone from this side or the other side will be moving down to try to get the gold." They all lay down in the grass and watched and waited.

Nearly ten minutes later they saw four figures move down the far bank. Jim waited until the men were half way down, and in the open on the bank.

"Stop them," Jim said. The men sighted in and on Jim's order they all fired. Then they fired when they were ready, and the four men going down the bank were soon silent as death on the side of the gorge two hundred yards away.

A noise attracted the guards and they looked behind them on the right of way and saw three horsemen thundering down toward them. All had pistols out and were firing.

"We've got friends to the rear," Jim said and pushed Mandy down and lay covering her as he fired at the oncoming horsemen.

It was no contest. The stationary riflemen could sight in well from a firm position, and their weapons had greater range. They blew two of the riders out of their saddles before they came into effective pistol range. The third man swung around and, lying close to the neck of his horse, rode away unscratched.

Jim surveyed the damage below in the gorge. The train still billowed steam, but there was no fire. He saw two horsemen on the far bank mount up and ride away, seeking cover quickly in the heavy brush. Jim moved his group to the end of the tracks and looked below again.

That was when Jim remembered the one live bushwacking, fake soldier they had left in the passenger car morgue. The man got what he bargained for, Jim decided. He was sure that no one could live through such a plunge.

They found Josh, Conductor Franklin and the brakeman at the end of the tracks looking downward. Gatling had remembered to dig out his emergency telegraph key from his gear before the train went over the side. Now he climbed a nearby telegraph pole with his kit and soon was tapping out word of the smashup to Denver and all points east and west. All traffic both ways would be halted until repairs could be made. The telegraph line went across the gorge on poles, not on the bridge, so the line had not been broken.

Gatling came down smiling. "The company says they will send a train to meet us on the other side of the break. We should proceed to Pine Valley on foot and wait for contact."

Jim motioned them to an old trail that led down this side of the cut.

"You go on into town, with Mandy. I'll send two men to bring back some supplies. We'll make a crutch for our guard with the broken leg and see if he can hobble back into town. Then I and the seven other guards will go down and check out the wreckage and post a guard around it until the railroad people get here. We'll leave just as soon as we get that gold safely on board the next train."

Jim looked at Mandy. "As for you, young lady . . ."

Mandy held up her hands in protest. "Now wait. You ordered me off the train, right?" Jim nodded. "And you did see me get off the train, correct?"

Jim said he did.

"But you absolutely did not tell me to stay in that little town, and you positively did not tell me that I could not get back on that silly little train before it left."

Jim shook his head, laughing. "You might think you won, but you haven't. We'll argue more about this when we get on into Denver. Now scoot into town and stay out of trouble."

CHAPTER 16

Three days later, Mandy Martindale and Jim Steel walked out of the United States Mint in Denver. Mandy carried a check for $502,694.40, complete payment for 152 gold bars. Jim hustled her directly to her father's Denver bank where the check was deposited.

Mandy wore a new light blue dress, a new hat and new shoes. She had been so excited when they arrived in Denver that morning that she let Jim take care of delivering, unloading, counting and weighing the gold, while she went to the Robinsons', the best women's store in town, and began buying clothes. She met Jim at the mint at noon for the presentation of the check.

At the bank she had fifteen thousand dollars transferred to Jim's account with a letter of authorization from her father. That covered Jim's wages. She drew a check for a thousand dollars and then found the Denver offices of the Union Pacific Railroad. They talked to the man in charge of personnel. Mandy demanded that Josh Flynn, the young fireman, be promoted to engineer at once, and that he be given a raise and a bonus for his exceptional work in taking the train when the engineer was murdered in California. She also asked for Josh's home address so she could mail him a reward check from the Lucky Seven Mining Company of Sacramento for his excellent work.

Back on the street Mandy held Jim's arm and giggled.

"Did you see the strange look he gave me when I demanded that Josh be promoted to engineer? I'll have Daddy send a letter and also demand the promotion. That will set their minds buzzing. I like Josh and he did a good job for us. Don't you think?"

"Yes, I agree," Jim said. "Now it's back to the hotel. You have to take your beauty nap, then I'll pick you up for the sightseeing tour I promised you this afternoon. Then we have dinner at the fanciest restaurant in town and tonight, the Denver Opera. You'll love the opera, its singing and dancing and wonderful costumes."

"Opera? I never liked it in San Francisco."

"You were very young then."

At the hotel she found a telegram from

her father. She opened it at once and read it, then showed it to Jim.

CONGRATULATIONS TO YOU BOTH STOP TELL JIM STEEL HE CAN WORK FOR US ON THE NEXT GOLD TRAIN STOP DON'T BUY ANY MORE DRESSES STOP ARMY ANGRY ABOUT AMBUSH STOP SEND GUARDS HOME ON NEXT TRAIN TO PINE VALLEY STOP SHUTTLE ACROSS BREAK STOP BUYING DRESSES STOP LOVE DADDY

The afternoon and evening were fascinating for Mandy. She watched everything, asked dozens of questions, and when Jim escorted her back to her room in the Denver House hotel, she wasn't ready for it to end. Her room was a dozen doors down from Jim's on the third floor. She paused at the door.

"I want to see your room, Jim," she said.

Jim shook his head. "That's not proper and you know it."

"To hell with proper. I want to see your room." She turned and walked down the hall to his doorway and stood there. He came up beside her.

"Are you going to kick the door down?" he asked. "It's locked and I have the key."

She smiled. "Jim, darling. Either you open the door right now, or I'll tear my dress half off and begin screaming and yelling that you've been trying to rape me. How will you get out of that one?"

He remembered her performance back at Sacramento. Here with a quick dozen witnesses she would put on a dramatic show. He would be lynched before midnight.

Jim reached down and unlocked the door.

She smiled and went inside the room, closed the door and locked it. Mandy smiled and put her arms around Jim's neck and kissed him, her mouth was open, her tongue darting.

"I've been wanting to get you alone for such a long time, Jim," she said. She giggled and led him to the bed where she sat down and pulled him down beside her. Mandy kissed him again, then pushed him until he fell on his back on the bed. At once she rolled over on top of him. She kissed him again but he made no move to respond. Mandy frowned, propped her elbows on his chest, her chin in her palms.

"Honestly, I don't know what's the matter with you, Jim Steel. You know I like you, and you kissed me on the train. But now you're acting like I'm your sister or something."

She reached down and kissed him again. "Maybe you think I'm too young. You know that I'm almost twenty. That's plenty old enough."

She wiggled on top of him, rubbing her breasts against his chest. Then she kissed him again and this time Jim kissed her back.

"Damn, but you are insistent. Is it true that rich girls always get everything they want?"

"Usually, but I thought for a minute there you were going to spoil everything." She unbuttoned the fasteners on the front of her dress and pulled it open so her breasts swung down toward him.

"You know it's going to be at least two weeks before they get that train trestle rebuilt out at Pine Valley," he said.

Mandy grinned. "I do know that. I tried to bribe them into taking three weeks," Mandy said. "Two weeks of dinners with you, and going out at night with you, and staying in our room in bed most of the day, just the two of us."

"Mandy, you're shameless."

"No, I've fallen in love, and I want you to love me for as long as you will, because I know one of these days you'll go riding off and all I'll have left of you will be my memories, my wonderful, marvelous, beautiful memories."

"Hey, you talk too much," Jim Steel said, and he began kissing her so she would have all those memories.

The employees of Thorndike Press hope you have enjoyed this Large Print book. All our Thorndike, Wheeler, and Kennebec Large Print titles are designed for easy reading, and all our books are made to last. Other Thorndike Press Large Print books are available at your library, through selected bookstores, or directly from us.

For information about titles, please call:
  (800) 223-1244

or visit our Web site at:
  http://gale.cengage.com/thorndike

To share your comments, please write:
  Publisher
  Thorndike Press
  295 Kennedy Memorial Drive
  Waterville, ME 04901